THE SATANIC CHAPEL
by
BOB PRICE

The characters and events portrayed in this book are fictitious. Any similarity to real persons, living or dead, is coincidental and not intended by the author.

ISBN-978-1-7396732-0-8 (e-book)

Cover design by: The Author

About the Author

Bob Price was born on the African continent to European parents back in the ‘50s. He travelled across the African continent and pretty much the whole of Europe before settling down in Northern Ireland. Where he now lives with his wife and four children. His work includes multiple genres that include crime, horror, political satire, science fiction, supernatural and westerns. An animal lover he has a variety of pets surrounding him including goats, ducks, cats, and dogs. As a petrol head he enjoys cleaning and driving his modern classics.

Summary

Believing yourself to be in a position to control the Devil has been the ambition of many Satanists over the centuries. None has yet proven successful because the Devil has his own agenda and knows exactly what people are about. Yet even in the twenty first century they continue to try ignoring the failures of the past at their own peril.

Members of The Satanic Chapel had reached a point of self-confidence when they too felt ready to take the next step. An invitation to the Devil himself to visit and help them rule the world of humans. It was an ambitious plan that was years in the making and now it was finally ready and wheels within wheels were moving to make it a reality.

TABLE OF CONTENTS

CHAPTER ONE

"Mr Burns we're detectives from the Serious Fraud Office. We'd like to ask you some questions pertinent to an investigation we're following." Harringay was a tall broad-shouldered detective with twenty years' experience. The lines on his face and intense dark eyes suggested he wasn't anyone to mess with. His partner Harry Davies was ten years younger but no less intimidating. Both wore face masks due to the COVID-19 pandemic even though it was no longer mandatory. A choice.

Arthur Burns, a small thin man with thinning brown hair stared back at the detectives through thick lensed spectacles. Unaccustomed to visits by the police he hoped none of his neighbours had seen them. Not that they were in uniform it was just obvious they weren't insurance salesmen. His property not grand was still sizeable. A detached corner property with a tall hedge encircling the grounds made the chances neighbours spotted his visitors less likely.

He led them into a large open plan kitchen diner where his wife Emily was cooking dinner. Neither wore a face mask. “I really don’t know of any reason I might be of help to the police.” His voice was high pitched with a squeaky resonance that reminded Harringay of mice.

His wife on the other hand was something completely different. A good-looking red head at least ten years younger with a fine figure neatly wrapped in blouse and skirt that neither detective missed. She looked familiar to Harringay, but he wasn’t sure where they might have met or why his usually perfect memory for faces was letting him down. Her surprise at hearing they were police obvious as she flicked off the cooker and moved round an island table to hear what they had say. Leaning a hip against it as if she were ready to spring to his defence if the need arose only helped accentuate her figure. Her voice was low and husky. The kind that caught attention without trying. “Can I get you gentlemen something? A tea or coffee?”

Both men nodded their thanks and asked for coffee before using the seats offered by her husband.

The open plan diner was dressed in modern furniture and fittings with a tiled patterned floor that looked new and glossy. Burns sat opposite the detectives separated by a long white table. His body language appeared nervous as he leaned forward elbows resting on its top hands clasped together. It wasn’t unusual for people who had little experience dealing with the police to behave that way, especially given the size of the two detectives and their gruff tones.

Harringay produced a slip of paper from an inside jacket pocket and handed it across the table. “Do you recognise any of the names or addresses listed?”

Burns studied a list of nine names. A deep frown creased his forehead indicating he was genuinely trying to recall them. “That’s me at the bottom.” He said finally uncertain what it might mean.

“It’s why we’re here,” Harringay said. “Do you recognise any other name?” Burns vigorously shook his head. “You all have one thing in common.”

“What’s that detective?”

“You’re all accountants.”

He looked surprised while reviewing the list a second time. “I might know them if I saw them, but their names mean nothing to me. Though I notice they all live in different parts of the country. I’m the only one who lives in London. There’s no reason I’d know any of them.”

"True," Davies said entering the conversation. "Yet you're also the only one doing something they're not."

Burns screwed up his face as if unable to guess.

"Breathing," Davies explained. "They're all dead."

When told bad news blood is known to drain from a person's face. Much the way it did from Burns. "Dead. How?"

"Two were victims of a hit and run. One drowned in his own bath. The other four hung themselves."

"Have you anything you might want to tell us Mister Burns? Harringay asked.

The little man shook his head, "I don't know anything."

"Why are you on this list?"

"I have no idea?" He shoulders gave an involuntary shudder that told its own story. An association with eight dead accountants on a list that included your name was bound to make anyone nervous.

"Would you tell us if you knew?" Davies asked.

"Of course he would," His wife piped up bringing their coffee to the table. As she leaned forward the vee of her blouse parted enough to reveal an ample cleavage. Something Davies noted while Harringay caught sight of a tattoo on the palm of her left hand. His expression gave away that he recognised it as his gaze looked up at her with refreshed curiosity.

She caught the change in his eyes and something more yet remained coolly detached, "My husband isn't a criminal."

"We never said he was," Harringay replied. "But he's on a list of dead men and that can't be good. You look familiar Mrs Burns have we ever met before today. I rarely forget a face?"

"I'm sure I'd have remembered if we had," she replied casually. "I've never had anything to do with the police in the past."

"I wish I could help you," Burns interrupted. "Really I do. I don't know why I'm on that list someone has made a terrible mistake. Do you think I'm safe?"

"Arthur tell them about the painting," his wife said.

He stared up at her with more than a hint of confusion before something triggered a memory. "The painting," he repeated. "Yes of course. I'd forgotten about that."

"What painting?" Harringay asked.

She stepped out of the room and returned a minute later carrying a twelve-by-twelve-inch oil painting that she handed to them. Harringay studied it for a moment. Wrapped in plastic sealed with Sellotape a thin wooden frame surrounded an oil painting depicting a black gated entrance into the side of a grey boulder mountain.

"What is this?" He asked.

"We don't know," she replied. "It arrived addressed to Arthur a few days ago. There was no return address."

"It looks old. Is this how it arrived, or did you package it up?"

"That's how it came. It was left on our doorstep. We never saw by who."

"Do you mind if we take this with us, we can have it checked for fingerprints?"

"Go ahead," she said. "We don't want it. It's a little creepy."

Davies wanted to bring Arthur Burns in for questioning, but Harringay had other ideas. "Okay Mister Burns well if you think of anything. Anything at all I want you to contact me." Handing him a business card he glanced at Emily Burns one last time in an effort to recall where he might have come across her. Those tattoos were not common, and neither was the good-looking red head. "Stay safe."

As they made their way back to their car Davies could feel the Burns eyes on his back before they turned out the gate and disappeared behind the hedge.

***

Commander Reginald Brandown entered Buick's office without knocking. "Morning Betty."

"Morning Commander," she replied remaining seated behind her desk. Recently promoted to Superintendent she was learning new skills relating to seniority as well as how to handle a new boss. Neither was proving easy. Buick, a mid-forties brunette with twenty years in the job was considered formidable by all previous line managers. Something her insistence at doing things her way when handed an investigation which often generated resentment from others, especially when she proved successful. Today, she had given up worrying about resentment long ago. However, that didn't prevent it from rearing its head as it usually arrived in a routine package of machismo obvious from body language and rhetoric. As was the case with her latest boss Commander Brandown ever since their first meeting just a week ago. He had eyed her from a distance before approaching her at a formal event. She had watched him throughout wondering when he would take the plunge and finally introduce himself. It took half an hour and when he stopped in front of her his entire being felt tense while communication was stilted and distant. That he had read her file was the second thing he told her after introducing himself. She could see the effect it had had on him which made her smile. Strong women sometimes did that to men, he wasn't the first and no doubt wouldn't be the last. She had lived with it all her career and so far had never allowed it to prevent her from making progress.

It was just four years ago she was invited to set-up a new form of missing persons unit. One that handled cases involving strange incidents far removed from the regular type of missing persons cases. Initially figuring she was being dumped on she reluctantly accepted the new posting since it came with a promotion to Chief Inspector. The Irregular Missing Persons unit (IMP) was formed with her and two other detectives, both with colourful backgrounds and on the verge of quitting. That felt like a long time ago as today IMP included another detective and uniformed officer. Its track record of successful investigations provided credibility among senior management while it was kept away from public scrutiny. With IMP located in the basement at New Scotland Yard its existence and unusual function were just where Buick wanted it. Out of sight and not easily stumbled into by pedestrian traffic.

Brandown did not smile as if to do so might do him some damage. In fact she couldn't recall ever seeing him exhibit pleasure. He was too serious to be influenced by amusing or frivolous activities. Additionally, her own research revealed that he was highly career minded and determined to be either a Chief Constable or Commissioner. She registered it to mean that he would crush anyone who got in the way of his aspirations.

He was a tall, neat man with a uniform so well pressed it was the envy of every probationer. The gloss of his black shoes gave them a mirror like appearance while short, cropped hair befitted that of a Royal Marine. “Finally have something to occupy your little team,” he said without sitting down. Preferring to move slowly round in front of her while speaking. “A couple of people have been reported missing within the past twenty-four hours.”

“That’s not very long, especially for us. Are you certain they haven’t simply decided to take an unscheduled trip?” She didn’t want to sound uninterested particularly as he had passed nothing down to IMP since his arrival.

"I very much doubt it," Brandown said pausing momentarily to meet her gaze. "A couple of detectives from the SFO. One whose wife is about to give birth to their third child the other divorced and not known for using his leave unless forced to do so. They're very much missing. We found their car outside the house of an individual helping them with enquiries. He's not a suspect but could well end up a victim."

"Are there any reasons to consider foul play at this stage?"

"No blood stains if that's what you mean," he said and began walking her office again. "But a couple of detectives would hardly have taken an unscheduled jaunt during the middle of an investigation would they?"

"In that case why have you come to me Commander. You know our speciality and if you believe the officers to be the victims of foul play then surely major crimes or one of the other departments would be better suited?"

He paused again complexion reddening, "There is something else." It had been clear when they first met that he was dubious about IMP and its relevance to police operations. The supernatural more to do with religion than policing but his doubts had been over-ruled. "The investigation they're involved is associated with members of the Satanic Chapel in the East End." Revealing that had in his own eyes cost him self-esteem. He had already warned her that he was an atheist and tried to downplay any evidence of the supernatural discovered in IMP investigations. By coming to her with this investigation he could not completely deny the possibility of supernatural interference which meant he was conflicted. Not that Buick was the type to make anyone feel bad for having a different opinion or even as she suspected because they did not like women. His insecurities clearly played a prominent part in how he managed IMP. She could only hope that it wouldn't prevent her from continuing to achieve the results she had already accomplished.

"Will you email me with all that you have, and we'll get to work on it immediately Commander."

"Just one more thing, "he said dryly. "You'll only be acting as a support unit to the officers already assigned the investigation." She should have expected it from him. This was the first investigation he had assigned IMP and his determination to be seen in the best possible light by senior management meant whatever he delegated to her would not easily fall back to him if it went pear shaped. With Buick acting simply as an adviser any fallout would not return their way. "Try not stepping on anyone's toes. The lead officer is Superintendent Marshal. You're there to offer advice if it's needed that's all."

"I see," she replied. "In that case I'll only need to take one of my officers with me. Thanks for making our role clear."

"Good," he replied suddenly delighted not having to explain the appearance of her entire unit to Marshal. "I'll email you as soon as I return to my office."

With that he left her alone.

As always she thought to herself we've been relegated to second place even with a case history that revealed the existence of supernatural entities impacting crimes. Buick strolled out to the team sitting at their desks reviewing cold case files searching for indications of supernatural interference.

. "We've just been asked to assist in an investigation purely in an advisory role. I'll be taking Toni with me," she said eyeing the detective sergeant. "If this suddenly turns into something we need to handle I want you ready."

The other three officers one in uniform nodded. DI Bran Maddox and DI Billy Hughes rose from their desk together.

Maddox wearing a frown, “Is the new Commander becoming accustomed to the idea that the supernatural is real.”

Buick had a relaxed relationship with all her staff but drew the line at openly criticising senior management in front of them. Maddox had also sensed Brandown’s anti-female characteristic viewing it far more indignantly than her boss. Also, as a strong supporter of female equality in the police she sometimes could not help herself from being outspoken. Buick stopped their conversation developing further, “He’s our boss and has his opinion. All we can do is teach him what we’re learning. It wasn’t easy to accept for any of us as I remember.”

Maddox shrugged.

Hughes, the only male detective seconded from British Transport Police nodded, “It certainly took me a face to face with a demon to realise they’re real.”

***

Superintendent Frank Marshal was lead officer of the Metropolitan Investigations Team (MIT) that specialised in homicides. Twenty-four MITs operate within the Metropolitan Police district meaning that those in charge have proven their ability to successfully lead and hunt down killers. When they arrived at the crime scene outside the Burns property. They quickly found the non-descript police car used by the detectives where it had been left by them. Taking the lead Buick introduced herself to the officer in charge.

“Nice to meet you Betty,” Marshal said behind a face mask. No shaking hands or bumping elbows. His eyes made his introduction. “I have to admit I’d never heard of IMP until today.”

"We keep a low profile," she smiled behind her own face mask. Marshal was genuinely friendly and curious. It was rare for a specialist team that he had never come across to support MIT. "As I'm sure our Commander informed you we're here to simply look at the evidence to ascertain whether our specialist knowledge might be of use."

"Yes, he told me, but never explained what that specialist knowledge might be?"

Just like Brandown she thought. Avoiding explanation and thereby putting her on the spot. He was so intent to avoid his career being marked by any stigma associated with the supernatural he refused to even explain the reason for IMP

Marshal was a seasoned officer who rose through the ranks same as everyone. A shrewd mind and willingness to push himself harder than others had ensured recognition and earned him his promotion.

Recognising Buick had issues with her Boss not great leap for him. "Does Brandown have a broomstick up his backside, because he certainly sounded like he did."

It sometimes doesn't take much to know that you and someone you just meet are on the same page. This was one of those times. She smiled, "You're so right."

"Yeah, know the type Betty. Look you can tell me what you're looking for or not. I won't be offended. If you do find something of interest that might help us, promise you'll let me know."

"Promise," she said.

He turned to stare at the police vehicle cordoned off by yellow tape. No blood no signs of damage everything looks perfectly okay. The last people to see them are the Burns who live in the house behind the tall hedge."

"Are they suspects?"

"Not really, but I don't completely rule them out. Truth is his name is on some kind of hit list. He's an accountant so there's a serious chance he was involved in something that causes a rich client or clients to feel threatened."

She nodded momentarily scanning the crowd held back by the police yellow tape. The usual suspects of reporters and cameramen together with the idly curious spectators always present at crime scenes. Many wearing face masks a few without. The one who caught her eye taller than any of them broader too, as big as Billy Hughes, maybe even a little taller. His eyes behind a face mask busily absorbing the scene in a way a professional would. When their gazes met a momentary exchange was enough for Buick to recognise more than passing interest. He turned away soon after strolling over to a dark car before leaving. She caught its registration number and made a mental note.

"Do you want to talk to the couple in the house?" Marshal asked.

"Only if it doesn't upset you?" She checked.

He smiled, "We have an agreement don't we?"

Burns and his wife were in a front room. Sitting close together on a sofa as Buick and Dukes joined them. Like the open plan kitchen the room was brightly painted with a modernistic feel. After introductions were made by Marshal left them alone.

"I don't understand we've already told other detectives everything we know," Emily Burns told them her left hand squeezing that of her husband's. "I'm beginning to feel that you suspect us of kidnapping your officers."

"We need to assure ourselves that you haven't unwittingly omitted telling us anything that you might not have previously considered relevant.

My team specialise in obscure. pieces of information to build a picture relating to what might have occurred. You see it appears that between your front door and their car parked outside your house our detectives vanished. Yet you claim to have watched them reach your gate and turn out of sight towards their car. That leaves very little distance for kidnappers to attack, and it is also unlikely that the detectives would have gone quietly which means you might have heard something without realising what it was."

Burns looked at his wife, who shook her head. "Not that either of us remembers."

"Would you like some tea," Emily Burns asked releasing her husband's hand and rising to her feet. "I find it difficult being still when nervous and need to keep myself busy."

"No thank you," Buick replied catching sight of the tattoo on her hand. Not that her expression showed any sign that she understood its significance. The sign revealed that she was a member of the Satanic Chapel. The colours of the tattoo denoting that she was at the very least a lector priestess. A Satanic religious writer second to a High Priestess. Her opinion of Burns wife immediately changed. The tattoo suddenly making her a potential suspect. It was common for members of the Satanic Chapel to maintain a low profile to the point of keeping what they were secret even from their partners. Fixing her gaze on Arthur Burns she resisted the temptation to watch what his wife did before leaving them.

Dukes was perceptive enough to recognise when something was bothering her boss. Uncertain what it might be other than Burns or his wife she remained silent spectating while her boss continued the interview.

"Have you any clients who asked you to do things that might be construed as illegal. Hiding money avoiding taxation, things like that?"

"People hire me to save them money but only if it's possible to do so legally. None of my clients consider me a threat, at least not for any reason I can think of."

With his hands resting on his knees the backs of them clear of any marks she felt satisfied that Arthur Burns might not be involved with the Satanic Chapel. Not wittingly anyway.

"How long have you been married Arthur?"

The question took him by surprise, "What has that to do with anything?"

"A little background information is useful," she replied.

"Ten years."

"Where did you meet?" Dukes asked.

He turned his attention to her, "She worked for a client. I was in a bad place at the time, and she lifted my spirits. It only took us a short while to discover that we had much in common. A few months later we married."

"Why were you in a bad place?" Buick asked.

Hesitating as words appeared to catch in his throat. "Julia my previous wife was killed in a motoring accident eighteen months before I met Emily."

"I'm sorry," Buick sympathised.

"She was my soul partner. I'd known her from our schooldays we were inseparable. I took her death very badly. I like to think Emily was a Godsend."

"I'm sure," Buick replied.

Once outside Dukes found herself suppressing her own curiosity as they sought out Marshal who was discussing things with a few officers. Quickly deducing from their body language they had something to share Marshal left his officers to join them. "How did it go?"

"Were you aware that his wife is a member of the Satanic Chapel?"

A deep frown crossed his brow, "Are you sure?"

"Yes," she replied. "She wears their mark on her left hand. They use the left side of the body for inscriptions because its nearest the heart."

"Okay," he replied. "What does that mean for my investigation?"

"The accountants on the list were all associated with the Satanic Chapel except for Arthur Burns. I suggest it's not a coincidence."

"I take it this is the speciality IMP deals with?" He asked eyes narrowed.

Buick nodded, holding her breath for his next reaction.

"In that case would you agree to continue enquiries in this specialised area?"

Not what she had expected but not bad either. "Of course."

"You'll obviously need to keep me up-to-speed with progress."

"Not a problem," she assured him. She liked Marshal from the outset and his willingness to permit her to investigate their specialised field of activity increased her admiration. It was a rare quality to encounter in a man's world especially considering the narrow-minded Commander who was her boss. "It may lead to nothing but if it does you'll be the first to know."

"Marshal seemed nice," Dukes said as she drove them back to the Yard. "Do you think the Burns woman is somehow implicated?"

"Without doubt," Buick firmly replied. "There's no such thing as coincidence all we don't yet understand is how she fits into her husband being on a hit list?"

"What about the missing detectives?"

"Maybe, but it's a lot murkier how she might be involved in their disappearance. That said, neither Burns come across as capable of overpowering two detectives."

"Not unless she has some superpower." Dukes replied. "If they were kidnapped there must have been a vehicle to take them away, but that doesn't explain why anyone would take them. I know Marshal will be scouring their files to identify a potential link between a crime they're investigating and their kidnap. Perhaps that's what this will end up being about, nothing to do with Burns or even the Satanic Chapel. Impossible to know at present."

At the office Buick issued instructions: "Helen, check this registration for me." She handed the uniformed constable a piece of paper with the registration of the vehicle being driven away by the big man at the crime scene. "After that dig out any information you can concerning the death of Julia Burns. She was killed in a motoring accident about twelve years ago. I'd also like you to check out an Emily Burns at the address we visited. Find whatever you can on both of them no matter how unimportant it might appear."

"Yes, mam," PC Helen Frobisher replied unable to prevent herself calling Buick Mam. Something Buick detested. "Sorry, Boss."

"You'll get the hang of it," she smiled. Turning to DI's Billy Hughes and Bran Maddox, "I need you two to visit the Satanic Chapel at Manor Park. It's in its own grounds and there's always someone on site twenty-four seven. Collect all vehicle registrations in the Chapel grounds we need to find an association with someone at the crime scene. I want you to ask whoever you meet what position Emily Burns has within the organisation."

"Are they likely to tell us?" Hughes asked rising from his desk to stand his full height of six feet four dwarfing them all.

"No idea," she replied. "But gauge their reaction to her name. If I'm right at least we'll have established her base of operation."

Turning to Dukes she asked, "Did you get their photos?"

"Yes Boss just sending them to the printer." Dukes followed a routine Buick introduced of taking photographs with her mobile of anyone they interviewed. The practice was clearly not included in the police handbook, but she figured it too useful. A Buick rule that might one day spark her to write her own handbook. For the time being only her team were aware.

"No offence Boss, but I thought we were only acting as advisers in this investigation?" Maddox asked.

"Fortunately, the lead officer appreciates our services better than some. He asked that we investigate the Satanic Chapel aspects and I agreed." Remaining indifferent when someone was proving to be purposely problematic required discipline and objectivity. Knowing that what you were doing was in the best interests of all paramount. Another Buick rule. It was how she handled disappointment with senior management. However, these days her disappointment appeared to be growing which was more than a little alarming. Maintaining standards had always been characteristic of her career. Certainly, she cut corners when necessary but never without justification that those immediately around her understood. She knew that did not make what she sometimes did right in the eyes of the law, but figured as long as no one got hurt and a rule was only bent rather than totally dispensed with her interpretation could be argued.

The uniformed constable joined them, “The vehicle registration you wanted me to check is a rental. The company says the cars was returned earlier. The user was a Martin Luther D.O.B: thirty-eleven-eighty-five. An American tourist. He’s staying at the Four Seasons Hotel Park Lane.”

“Thanks Helen,” Buick said before turning to Dukes. “We’re going to pay him a visit and see how the other half lives. Bran you and Billy visit the Chapel at Manor Park. We'll meet back here when we're done."

***

The Four-Seasons hotel at Park Lane was used by a wealthy clientele able to afford the cost of cossetting. People accustomed to being pampered saw the world through different eyes. These days those eyes had moved so far from reality she wondered if they were ever likely to return. Approaching the entrance the door was pushed open by a doorman wearing a bright smile that suggested he was happy. No face masks. The virus not expected to reach beyond the entrance. However, if he had been expecting a tip he must have been disappointed as they stepped inside without a second look. Reception was like a sanctum. A very rich sanctum with marble floor, red walls occupied by oversized oil paintings, leather furniture and what was possibly the longest mahogany reception desk they had ever seen.

As Buick always felt when entering such places a sense of indulgence and grandeur designed to impress usually fell flat. Maybe it was her, but she figured grandeur overrated. The rich enjoyed flaunting their wealth to those less fortunate in this instance the hotel staff. Also, the stench of cleanliness was incredibly powerful as the morning shift of cleaners repeated cleaning what their shift predecessors had already cleaned. It was a twenty-four-hour routine cycle meant to demonstrate to the guests they were safe from the virus because of all the effort put into cleaning all the fixtures, floors, and furniture. The aroma of floor wax wafting in every direction making even the air taste scrubbed. She knew of some hospitals that could have done with the hotel's standard of cleanliness. A grey marble floor stretched out on all sides as they paused to look around. To their left and right leather seating ahead the long reception desk with several receptionists wearing the same bright smile as the doorman. So much reliance on the virus not finding its way to the reception desk was not sufficiently comforting for either Buick or Dukes not to wear their face masks.

Of more concern to Buick was the possibility staff would be overly disappointed by her resistance to tipping as a common courtesy.

"How may I help you?" A receptionist with the name tag Pam asked. Her bright smile fixed to her pretty face as if glued. Buick made the introductions and asked for Luther's room number. She checked a computer screen and within a minute informed them Luther had already booked out.

"He's not hanging about," Dukes muttered.

"We need to take a look in his room," Buick said.

It appeared no expense had been spared. Luther's room was on the 9th floor in one of the newly modelled single bedroom suites that offered sweeping views of London. Modern furnishings were tasteful while the room itself was spacious and included a living and dining area.

Digging deep into her satchel Buick removed a pair of magnifying glasses to study all areas likely to contain fingerprints. The maid had not yet arrived, and Luther's bed was rumpled while everything else seemed untouched. When finished she returned the eyeglasses to her satchel. "Everything's been wiped clean. Not a single print anywhere not even in the bathroom."

"A professional of some sort," Dukes added.

"Seems so," she replied and used her mobile to contact Marshal. "Hi Frank, I might have something for you. I spotted a man at the crime scene this morning and ran a number plate. I didn't give it much thought until now. The vehicle was a rental and the individual had been staying until a little while ago at the Four Seasons in Park Lane. The name he's using is Martin Luther. American, white about six feet five and very broad, could be a wrestler. I think he spotted me spotting him but didn't say anything earlier because I wasn't sure. Now I am. We're in his hotel room and it's the cleanest I've ever come across. Not a single print anywhere. Everything has been wiped down even before the maid is due to arrive. I'll text you all the details we have."

"Thanks Betty I'll pass it onto my team," he said. Then in a softer tone, "I've been thinking. You and I should get together I'd like to know a little more about IMP. Perhaps dinner?"

Buick suddenly reddened caught off guard but his intimate tone, "Certainly, but I warn you I may have to kill you if I let too much slip."

“I’ll take my chances,” he chuckled. “I’ll be in touch and thanks again.”

“Are you alright Boss?” Dukes asked noting the hue of her complexion. “He didn’t have a go at you did he?”

“I suppose that’s one way of putting it,” she replied regaining composure.

***

The Satanic Chapel was close to the tube station. Built within its own grounds overlooking the railway line from a high embankment that reduced the sound of passing trains. The surrounding perimeter fence was wooden about six feet in height Just low enough for Hughes to see over the top. The Chapel was painted white and black with stained glass triangular upside-down windows. The stained glass adorned with a variety of vivid demonic images.

“You have to admit chasing ordinary villains is dull compared to insane people with demons." Hughes said from beneath his face mask.

"If I could go back to a time when I didn't think such things existed I would," Maddox remarked as they approached a pair of closed double doors. She used a large brass knocker to gain attention. A muffled deep resonating thud echoed audibly behind the doors.

"Wow, that sounded out of a Hammer House of Horrors movie," Hughes said.

"Then let's hope Dracula remains locked in the basement," she replied.

One of the doors swung inwards as a tall woman dressed in black appeared, "The Chapel is closed." Her accent distinctly foreign perhaps Germanic. No face mask allowed her perfect set of white teeth to be shown off together with sharp attractive features. Her dark eyes gazed with a kind of intimidation that was subtle yet obvious.

Hughes almost jumped out of his skin which for a man his size looked odd, even to Maddox. With the hackles on the nape of his neck fully extended he backed away a few steps as if she were about to pounce. Whatever passed between them invisible to the human eye enough to make the big man ready for a fight.

Maddox attempted to ignore his reaction by making the introductions and asked about Emily Burns.

The woman's expression remained neutral while her alabaster complexion caught the Sunshine as she stepped further out keeping the door close behind her. A fresh pink glow highlighted her sharp features and unusually long nose. Hughes frowned as if half expecting her to burn up in front of his eyes.

"Emily Burns hasn't been here in a while," She said turning her attention to Maddox.

"But she is a er……."

"A Satanist," the woman completed her sentence for her. "Yes, I have no reason to believe she has changed her views."

"How long has she been a Satanist?" Hughes asked moving cautiously forward prepared to defend himself. A sense of danger engulfing him as if an unearthly hand were tugging at his soul. His throat dry palms wet he adjusted his jacket as it were making him hot even his breath felt warmer than usual. What was it about this woman? Ever since his last encounter with a demon when the creature had almost pulled his head from his shoulders things had been different. His senses more acute. Dreams more vivid. Trying to figure what made the woman so repugnant

too clouded for him to comprehend. Maybe it was her scent a mixed aroma of musk and something he couldn't identify.

"I have no idea. I'm fairly new here myself," she said staring back at

Hughes as if sensing his revulsion. "I immigrated from Germany a year ago."

"Transylvania?" He muttered.

"Berlin," she corrected. "I don't think that I can help you any further. I have things to do."

"May we come inside to take a look around?" Maddox asked.

"We are a private members only organisation. Unless you have a search warrant I must decline." She remained blocking their access and Maddox figured it not worthwhile pushing this time around.

"You certainly seem to understand UK police procedures for someone who has only been in the country a year," Hughes said.

"I watch too much television. There are plenty of police shows." Her eyes held onto Hughes as if peering into his soul.

"Thank you," Maddox said. "If we need to return we will."

The woman backed against the door and inside keeping her gaze fixed on the big man as she did. The door closing quietly as she disappeared.

"You seem to have made a new friend," Maddox said as they turned away her mobile in hand photographing two vehicles parked in the grounds.

"Do you think the monster woman is watching us?" Hughes asked.

"I'd bet money on it, and I don't gamble."

***

As arranged they all met up in Buick's office occupying seats around her desk. She detailed what occurred in relation to the big American and finished by telling them he was no longer of concern to them as Marshal had taken on including him in his investigation. Buick then turned her attention on Maddox and quickly became fascinated by what had occurred at the Satanic Chapel with Hughes.

Hughes glanced at her, "The woman we encountered was odd. Don't ask me how or why but she is definitely odd"

The DCI's eyes narrowed as she repeated, "Odd. Not good enough Billy. I need a better explanation than that!"

"I sensed we were in danger."

"She and Billy hit if off straight away," Maddox grinned. Buick looked at him. "Lucky I was there otherwise I'm not sure who'd have won had they come to blows."

"And I thought you were our gentle giant," Dukes said.

"What's going on Billy?" Buick asked. "I don't recall you ever claiming to have sensed danger in the past?"

He had kept the secret long enough. It was not the kind of thing anyone could hold within themselves long. Those around him were the only ones he could share it with who would not consider him insane. His only problem that he had kept it to himself for a month. They were meant to mention if any of them felt different in anyway as soon as aware. "I've been having odd sensations."

"What kind of odd sensations?"

"Hard to explain but I seem to get a heightened nervous reaction when I get close to some people."

"You mean this has happened before today?" Maddox asked.

"Since the demon almost pulled my head off."

"That was a month ago!" she exclaimed. "Why didn't you tell us before now?"

Buick raised a hand to interrupt, "How many times has it happened since it began?"

"At least three including today," he replied. "I didn't say anything because I wasn't sure until today. The other times I was in the car driving slow passing pedestrians. It was impossible to be definite about what was happening to me. Then today with that woman I have no doubts."

“You must tell us when you feel these sensations again,” she said before turning to Maddox. “Did you manage to get a photograph of her?”

Maddox nodded, “It’s not very good,” she said passing her mobile over. “It was taken from my handbag looking up. I guess we can agree that she has a big nose from that angle.”

Hughes glanced at it, “She wanted to kill us.”

“You sound certain,” Buick said.

“I am,” He replied. “I felt it long and hard as if she were talking to me.”

“We need to revisit the Chapel this time with a warrant,” Buick said. “Whatever happened to Davies and Harringay doesn’t sound natural. Until we discover otherwise I intend keeping our investigation focused on the supernatural where they’re concerned. Right now Emily Burns seems significant because she’s a high-ranking priestess at the Chapel. What that makes her husband or how he fits in remains speculative at best.”

"Don't forget the dead people on the list Marshal shared were all accountants too. I don't think we should totally rule out Arthur Burns involvement," Maddox said.

"Did you find anything useful about his previous wife?" She asked Frobisher.

The uniformed officer nodded, "I'm still collecting data. It appears that his wife was killed in a motoring accident by a hit and run driver. No one was ever caught for the accident."

"Were they certain it was an accident?"

"It was recorded as such," she replied. "He met his present wife a few months later and the rest is history."

"Convenient," Dukes said. "Life doesn't usually work so well for people after losing a partner.

Buick nodded, "Remove an obstacle and replace it with one of their own. The Satanic Chapel might think Arthur worthwhile but why?"

"We need to know who his clients are as well as the clients of the dead on the list. Get on that will you Helen. The sooner the better."

Frobisher nodded. "I also checked the registrations of the two vehicles at the Satanic Chapel." She said handing a piece of paper to Buick.

"That's odd," she said. "The Ford Focus is registered to Emily Burns. I thought this woman said she hadn't seen her in a while?"

"I guess she lied," Hughes said unsurprised.

"The second vehicle is registered to a Philip Dang who lives in Manor Park."

"Isn't his surname Chinese?" Maddox asked.

"Could be, or Korean or Vietnamese. It's definitely Asian." Buick said. "Bran I'd like you and Billy to pay Mister Dang a visit see what he knows about Emily Burns. Toni, I want you to get me all you can on the Satanic Chapel at Manor Park. Call the locals see what they know as well as what's online. We need as many names as you can get."

Left alone Buick pondered what Hughes had told them and if it was possible that somehow he had been passed an ability from the demon who had almost killed him? If he did indeed possess a capability that identified supernatural entities occupying humans how had it been triggered? How did his physical body adapt itself to accommodate this new sense? What was the psychological impact on Hughes himself? The knowledge that the supernatural was real often hard enough to absorb for most. What troubled her with Hughes was what else might have transferred from the demon since he alone had made actual physical contact. Without wishing to heighten any personal fears he might not be sharing she phoned a surgery to arrange for Hughes to be examined.

CHAPTER TWO

Hughes was glad to have shared what was happening with him, whatever it might be? Trying to figure it out for himself not easy. Sitting beside Maddox in the car as the sky slipped into darkness he sat quietly watching pedestrians moving either side maybe hoping to feel a sensation that indicated someone unusual. As he did so Maddox occasionally glanced in his direction taking her eyes off the road as if checking for changes.

"Are you okay?" She asked finally unable to maintain the silence.

"I think so," he said. "Now that I've told everyone about my new sense, I'm not feeling a thing as we pass all the shoppers. Maybe telling you about it negated the power."

"Or maybe it's because they're normal," she said. "You only react to the abnormal. It's a gift, probably something unintended but your encounter with that demon may have provided us with a weapon that helps us find them."

He grinned, "People call people with unusual senses gifted like in the movies. I'm not so sure I agree. If I'm honest it makes me nervous."

She frowned, "Big guy like you nervous?"

"Discovering the truth about the supernatural functioning among us as we go about our daily lives makes me nervous. It's like we're monitored while supernatural entities wait their chance to reach in and cause chaos." He shifted on the seat turning to her, "I like to think I'm in control of my own life, but knowing the supernatural is so close and that it can dig into our reality as easily as it seems able makes me think our control isn't as strong as I previously thought."

"Wow, that's deep," she said. "But they can't reach us without help from people on this side. Well, not as far as we've experienced to date.

"How do you deal with knowing the supernatural is real?"

Maddox recalled the first time she discovered the truth. It was terrifying. More than she could ever have imagined, but she fought her fears and treated the supernatural as she would any villain. Giving them a label which differentiated between them. The type that had attacked Hughes were murderers there were others much smaller that were tricksters, illusionists that she classed as fraudsters. Somehow doing so helped her deal with them as well as the fact they too were vulnerable and not immortal and able to be sent back to wherever they came from. That was powerful knowledge as was the fact that the harmonics in the Lord's prayer offered a defence against most. If not killing them at least keeping them from killing her. "You never stop being terrified."

It was a statement of fact nothing more. He nodded, "I used to think nothing could ever scare me that much, but I was wrong."

"You and me both," she added. It was clear that Hughes was troubled perhaps because he used to view himself as some kind of protector. Typical of a big man. No doubt that version of him had taken a serious dent in its ego and needed to be reappraised. "How do you sleep at nights?"

"Not well, is that normal?"

"To be honest you're the first to make physical contact with a demon so what's happening to you may be different than the rest of us. Has Buick suggested you talk to a doctor?"

"No, does she think I'm losing it?" He asked.

Shaking her head she replied softly, "I know she thinks we all need to discuss with a psychologist what we're discovering. It's no small thing to discover monsters are real."

"I guess when you put it like that it makes sense," he looked at the pedestrians again. Most headed home after a day's work. Few had the time to stop and look around for monsters lurking in the bodies of those surrounding them, even if they could identify them. "Knowing what we do certainly makes the world feel like a more dangerous place than any of us realised."

"Don't over think about the demons and the Devil," she said. "They're natural to the universe if not our reality. Viewing them from that perspective makes them less threatening."

"You're very cool," he said. Admiring how she remained calm while able to discuss what terrified her.

"I've been doing this longer than you, that's all and had more time to accept the unacceptable. Also, Buick has helped. She understands what we're thinking because she dealt with her own demons before us."

"Can't have been easy for her."

"She had help from the Church."

"The Church?"

"Rome. Doesn't get higher than that."

"Do you believe in God?" He asked.

It was a question she had asked herself often enough after encountering her first demon. Even now she couldn't help herself shudder at the memory of its scaley face and body. If it had reached her she had no doubt she would be dead. It hadn't thanks to Buick who had sprung to her defence reciting the Lord's prayer and spraying it with Holy water. Who'd have guessed. The damn thing ran off faster than a heartbeat. Back to God. "The way I look at the world these days is more skewered than it used to be but that said, I'm inclined to believe if there are bad guys, that means there must also be good guys. It's all about balance and if the one thing this universe does daily is balance itself."

"I'll take that as a yes," he replied.

The Dang's lived in Manor Park a few miles from the Satanic Chapel. In a three bedroomed end of terrace property that backed against the underground rail lines that ran from Central London to Upminster in Essex. Their property had cars parked outside that probably belonged to neighbours except one which Hughes spotted.

"That was parked at the Chapel when we were there earlier."

"Yes," Maddox said. "It's how we came to be here. I wonder if that means Dang was at the Chapel when we visited?"

She used a doorbell they could hear ring inside and waited patiently for the front door to swing open. Mister Dang was a short rotund Asian with a swarthy complexion and balding aged around forty.

"Yes?" He asked wearing an uncertain smile.

No face mask Maddox thought ensuring her own covered her nose and mouth before she led with the introductions and questions about Emily Burns. "When was the last time you saw Emily?"

"A few days ago. She visited the Chapel with her husband. It was a first for him I think. He seemed nervous but soon got over his nerves when he discovered what a friendly bunch we all are."

She nodded, "Did she leave her car parked at the Chapel for a reason?"

"Too much to drink," he said. "We had wine and they both drank. One of our members gave them a ride home."

"What do you do as a job Mister Dang?" She asked.

"I'm an accountant," he said with a smile.

"Who is it Philip?" A female voice asked before the woman from the Chapel they had met earlier suddenly appeared behind him. She and Hughes spotted one another and even Maddox could feel an energy pass between them. "What are you doing at my home?"

Hughes stood his ground allowing a sensation of hatred to wash over him. The woman's face with its sharp angular features lit from behind smearing her in blurry shadows. Not a good look. Blinking repeatedly as her silhouette blurred and altered. To what he couldn't judge. Wider, darker something not of this Earth. Glancing at Maddox beside him as if expecting her to see the shape shifting creature in front of them. She appeared as confused as Dang whose uncertain expression suggested he was considering slamming the door shut.

"Are you alright?" Maddox asked.

He could only stare at her while struggling to find the words to reply.

"I apologise my partner is unwell, thank you for your time." She led him away by the arm back toward their car.

He slid silently onto the passenger seat and sat still while waiting for her to climb in next to him.

"What happened?"

He swivelled on the seat to look at her his voice lost someplace he couldn't find. Mute all he could do was stare back.

"Why aren't you speaking?"

Shaking his head he gestured to his voice box.

"Are you telling me that you've lost your voice?"

A nod enough confirmation.

"Did that bitch do this to you?"

He nodded.

"Does it hurt?"

His head shook.

"We're returning to the office, but first I'm going to call Buick." She lifted her mobile from a jacket pocket and pressed a button. It rang once before being answered. "Hi Betty, something has happened to Billy. He lost his voice."

"Good," a shrill voice replied. Not Betty Buick.

She swung the mobile from her ear to view its screen which remained

black. "Betty are you there?"

The talon that emerged from the screen was long black and curved at the tip. It didn't penetrate the skin as it touched her hand making her scream and jump with fright. "What the…" The mobile dropped to her lap.

"Stay away from the Dangs," the shrill voice said. "Stay away!"

"Hello, Bran. Are you there?" Betty Buick's familiar tone suddenly broke the momentary silence.

Maddox collected the mobile off her lap carefully turning it over to see an image of Buick staring back.

"Are you okay?" Buick asked.

"I... I think so," she replied. "We're on our way back."

"I heard you say something was wrong with Billy?" She said.

"No," he suddenly said. "I'm fine now."

Maddox didn't know what to say.

"See you soon," Buick said before the connection broke.

"What happened to you, one minute you're mute the next you're okay?" Maddox sounded angry.

"Why did you drop your mobile?" He replied.

Her hesitation said more than if she had replied. "Something odd is going on."

"Did you hear the voice tell us to leave the Dangs alone?"

"Couldn't miss it," he said looking at the Dangs house. "Did you see the woman go all blurry before looking like something else?"

"No I must have missed that part," she frowned. "What did you see, a demon?"

"Not like any we've encountered previously," he said.

"Then it wasn't a demon."

"Then what was it and how did it make me lose my voice?"

"I have no idea to both questions," she said starting the car and driving quickly away.

***

Buick listened intently as they both told their stories in her office. While Dukes and Frobisher appeared uncomfortable at the possibility they could be reached by the supernatural via their mobiles.

"Do you think we need to get close to them to infect your mobile?" Dukes asked.

"They can materialise through any reflective material," Buick said.

"Any?" Dukes frowned her mind racing with possibilities.

"Yes," she said. "Distance means nothing don't ever consider it a defence. We are all vulnerable to this, but I'm interested that we have been told to leave the Dangs alone. To me that means the Dangs are pivotal in regards what's happening."

"Are there any extra precautions we can take to prevent our mobiles being used as a demon doorway?" Dukes asked.

"I've already contacted the church and a priest is on his way. I'll leave that side of things to him. In the meantime we need to learn as much as we can about the Dangs. I need you all to work on that until Father O'Malley arrives."

Maddox the sensation of the talon against her hand still present remained behind. "Do you think we're able to deal with this?"

Buick looked up from her desk, "Close the door." After it closed she remained standing as the DCI continued. "We never know if we're able to deal with anything that we investigate. So far we have always been successful which must say something about our abilities."

"We've been lucky," Maddox said.

"What's going on Bran?" It was unusual for Maddox to waver. Buick had come to expect her to be a staunch supporter dealing with any supernatural threat. The fact she was now questioning their ability to do so totally unexpected.

"We're police officers rather than priests."

"True but our job is to protect the public which is what we do."

"It's just that the public have no idea what's out there. Maybe if they did we'd feel less helpless when something new shows up."

"You want this unit to go public?" She asked unable to conceal her surprise.

"If anything happens to any of us because of a supernatural entity no one including our families will ever know the truth."

"Do you want out?" Buick was never judgemental. She simply understood why any of her team might choose to return to ordinary duties. As far as she was concerned it was their choice. None could ever speak about what they had learned during their time at IMP, and she felt confident none would ever breach that condition.

"Do you think we're doing God's work?"

Knowing Maddox was not religious made her question all the more surprising. "Okay, now I'm intrigued what's going on with you?"

"Billy and I were talking, and he set me thinking. I notice that you always contact the church when beginning an investigation and I just wondered if the church is behind us doing these investigations."

"As you know they provide support what did you think?"

"I mean I've always believed in universal balance. If there's good then there has to be bad, that type of thing."

Buick nodded, "Okay, I'm following you so far."

"Well, it struck me that behind the bad guys is Satan. Therefore it makes sense that behind the good guys must be God." She waited for Buick to comment but the DCI remained silent. “I would like to know if Father O’Malley has ever mentioned that what we’re doing is on his behalf?”

“Not directly,” she replied. “Although I’m not sure what you’re getting at?”

“If God exists why isn’t he more visible, why is he leaving this to us?”

“You think he should be fighting demons beside us?”

“I think he should be putting in more of an appearance.”

“What do you want me to do send him an invite?” Buick was immediately annoyed with herself at being flippant. “I get it Bran. The talon that touched you has made you question what we do. It must have been terrifying. I’ve been there same as you.”

“I thought only Billy had made physical contact with demons. You never told me you’d experienced something like that?”

“It happened before IMP. I was a teenager. Fourteen or fifteen. At the time I lived in the country in Essex. My parents were out. I was meant to be doing school homework but chose to watch a video someone had given me. I'm still not sure whether it was the best or worst thing I've ever done."

"What happened?" Maddox sat down opposite.

"An entity came out of the TV from the video. Not a demon a Devil Worm. It moved faster than anything I had ever seen before and attached itself to me without actually penetrating my skin. I passed out on the floor and came round with my parents waking me. No sign of the worm or the video remained."

"Who gave you the video?"

"Another pupil, but she denied ever giving it to me. In the end the school and my parents believed her and figured I suffered some kind of concussion that affected my memory. Since then I've been able to magnify the effectiveness of the harmonics that apply to the Lord's prayer. It allows me to escape harm and to protect others."

"Have you ever come across God?"

A knock at the door heralded the arrival of Father O'Malley. The priest wearing a light mac covered in rain as he entered with a briefcase held in on hand. His dark greying hair flattened to his scalp as he wiped a tissue over his face. Pulling down a face mask revealed a trimmed beard and a good set of white teeth. "Sorry to interrupt but I have another visit to reach in less than an hour." His rich Irish accent as obvious as the nose on his face. While his age was difficult to guess between forty-five and fifty-five was Buick's guess.

"No problem Father," Buick told him. "I can get someone to drive you if that helps?"

"It would," he smiled. "You can have my humble company a little longer."

"Good. Do you mind if DI Maddox remains?"

"Not at all," he slipped out of the mac and hung it on a wall hook before taking over a seat alongside Maddox with the briefcase resting on his lap. "I can help you with what you told me about the creatures you encountered." His positive tone lifted their spirits for the first time that day. "You appear to be confronting an Illegra. A dark spirit that has the ability to take human form rather than possess a human."

"You mean it can live in our reality?" Buick asked.

"If an Illegra can reach our reality it has that ability. However, its lifespan is shorter than that of an ordinary human, though we have no idea by how much."

"You said if it can reach our reality, is that a problem for them?" Maddox asked.

"Yes, alternative realities have barriers to keep us separated. In truth we should never be permitted to transfer between them. However, evil will keep coming for us because they ignore the rules of the universe."

"And what about God?" Maddox asked.

O'Malley hesitated momentarily, "What about God?"

"Do you see us as doing his work?"

"Anyone who opposes evil is doing his work DI Maddox." He said eyes narrowing as he studied her before adding. "Do you have a problem with God?"

"Not with him. I want to know why he isn't visibly helping us?"

"Why do you think he isn't doing that?"

"Because I and my colleagues face these monsters alone. No one stands alongside when they attack us."

"You are quite wrong," O'Malley replied. "Whenever you confront evil God is present. Why do you think the Lord's prayer is powerful enough to defend you, it's because he provides it with the energy to do so. Without his help even the Lord's prayer would prove ineffective."

Maddox leaned back on the seat while her mind grappled with the possibilities of his response. "What happens when one of us dies or is injured, does that mean he deserted us at the moment we needed him most?"

"He would never do such a thing. Injuries and death are common traits of human mortality. They occur when fated to happen. That makes God's plan impossible for us to easily follow. We need faith that he knows what is for the best. That is what faith is about. Our lives are intentionally short in order that our spirits can return sooner."

Maddox frowned deeply the creases on her brow forming deep ripples. "Having faith is pretty tough Father."

"It needs to be," he said. "If it's truly genuine it has a power of its own.

The stronger the more powerful it is and the more powerful your defences are against evil."

Buick gave them both a moment before interrupting, "Do you have something we can use against the Illegra?"

"They move around in hives of no less than a hundred or more. It's one of the reasons they have difficulty crossing to our reality. The fewer that get here the less time they have to accomplish whatever it is they have come to do."

"A hundred!" Maddox exclaimed. "You mean we're facing an army of these things?"

"Yes," he replied.

"How do we kill them?"

"Like all supernatural beings they're not invulnerable." Reaching into the briefcase he removed four long blades of silver. "These have been blessed. You must strike at their heads to stab their brain. Also, they need to feed on human spirits.

Wherever they congregate you should notice an increase in the death rate usually among the homeless. The deaths will appear as a heart attack."

"What happens to the Illegra bodies after we kill them?" Maddox asked.

"They disappear in a cloud of black mist that returns to their reality."

"Is there another alternative to killing them?" Buick asked.

"If you find the way they accessed our reality and destroy it you will remove the entire hive in a single blow. They need the access open to maintain an energy stream to keep their human shape."

"How do we find it?"

"It must be located on sacred ground among the dead."

"You mean a cemetery?" She asked.

"Yes. You need to find a specific grave. Most commonly it will belong to a dead female who was a witch."

Buick stood up and walked round her desk, "The Satanic Chapel at Manor Park in the East End may be involved."

O'Malley nodded face grave, "They would not use a local cemetery, it would be too obvious. Expect them to travel some distance from the Chapel, perhaps even outside of London. Somewhere that a hundred strangers would go unnoticed."

"Do they automatically transform into humans upon arrival?" Maddox asked.

"It's possible for them to switch between what they are and the human form they take while here."

"Are they physically stronger than us?" Maddox asked.

"They are and have the power of telekinesis to back themselves up. If at all possible try to avoid physical contact."

Maddox immediately wished he had not said that. "Too late," she said.

“One touched me with its nail. It came out of my mobile.”

“Did it cut you?”

“No,” she said. “Is that good?”

“Better, not good.”

“Okay, I need to know what it means,” her tone a notch higher than usual. Being terrified did not however mean she was irrational in fact quite the opposite. Her external composure remained calm while inwardly she fought off an urge to surrender to a wave of dread that swept over her. “What am I likely to experience?”

“Which hand did it touch?” He asked.

“What?”

“Which hand did it touch?”

“My right, but what does it matter?”

“You’re left would have meant it intended to attack your health.”

“And my right?” She asked before he could finish.

“It’s using you as a beacon to know where you are at all times. As you have been warned off the Dangs I suggest they are involved in something quite dangerous. You were warned off to stop you discovering what that is."

"Do you have any idea what it might be Father?" Buick asked.

"It's very rare for a hive to slip through a portal. The last time it happened was in Five Three Six AD. A year in which the world suffered the worst weather ever experienced over the past two thousand years. Also, Italy was invaded by Belisarius who lay siege to Naples and a month later captured it. He then went on and entered Rome through Porta Asinaria which made the Gothic garrison of four thousand flee for their lives. Belisarius was victorious because he arrived in Rome with more than five hundred Illegra. However, when finished with their support he destroyed their portal and all five hundred were never seen again."

"Until now?"

"Why would anyone want them here?"

"They are able to help an individual who calls them to achieve a goal. They are chameleons or illusionists being able to swop from human appearance to their terrifying own in a matter of seconds. Together with their superior strength, ability to absorb souls and telekinesis they are a truly formidable adversary. I can only speculate why they have come it will likely be in support of a very powerful intrusion from another Dimension. Whoever has called to them from our reality will no doubt appreciate the dangers doing so brings with it. Therefore we must assume that either the Satanic Chapel or another such group are responsible."

"Have you any idea where they might have accessed our reality, even an inkling?" Buick asked.

"The best I can offer is it has to be somewhere thinly populated and as I have already said on sacred ground.

A cemetery. Your best way of locating them will be from a spike in the number of homeless dead. I wish I could help you more, but it will take me time to speak to all the resources available to me."

"How often do they need to feed?" Buick asked.

"Once a week at the very least," he said rising from the seat after closing his briefcase. "I must go."

She nodded and followed him into the outer office, "Toni I need you to take Father O'Malley to meet with someone." After the Father had gone she turned to Maddox who had returned to her desk. "For the moment Bran I want you to remain here with Frobisher."

"I guessed you'd say that."

"We can't take the risk they're using you to monitor our investigation. By remaining here they won't know where the rest of us are. What I need you to do is find out where that spike in the number of homeless dead is, then we can work out the rest."

CHAPTER THREE

The attack against the UK parliament came on a Wednesday when the Prime Minister was in attendance for Prime Minister Questions (PMQs). The hundred and fifty well-armed raiders wore black balaclavas and clothing. Encircling the House of Commons their main force used the river to land ashore from a flotilla of powerboats and quickly overwhelmed a thinly numbered unit of armed police. Hand to hand fighting with any who attempted to fend them off were similarly quickly dealt with as bodies drained of life fell aside. Visitors and staff workers meanwhile were herded together as the raider leader entered the debate chamber full of government and opposition Members of Parliament (MPs). An unfamiliar silence abruptly fell across the whole House as the attackers strode towards the Speaker weapons ready.

“You will stand down,” the leader said in a shrill high-pitched tone.

“It is not for you to demand I stand down. You have entered our Parliament……” He wasn’t given time to say more before the leader sucked his soul and threw his body aside as if garbage. Replacing him on the stand he addressed the politicians.

“Bow before me!”

No one moved some because they did not know what to do others because they stubbornly refused and some simply preferring to follow the example of those around them.

More raiders entered the chamber coming to a halt in front of their leader who barked a shrill indistinguishable order. A single raider stepped towards the government side selecting a female MP on the front bench. Taking her hand while pulling her gently to her feet she stood a foot shorter as they faced each other.

"Bow to our Lord," the raider said in an equally shrill tone.

"Never," the MP said.

The attacker leaned his face down towards her and sucked her soul. Its white misty essence visible to all as it transferred to the balaclava covered raider.

"This will happen to each of you until you kneel before me," the leader said.

No one moved. No one spoke. It was the quietest the House of Commons had ever been with a full contingent of MPs present.

Betty Buick awoke with a start from a troubled sleep. The memory of the government under attack a nightmare that remained vivid longer than any she had ever previously experienced. Climbing from the bed she wandered into the bathroom and ran the cold tap on the basin throwing water on her face to clear her head. Looking up at herself in a wall mirror she realised her nightmare had been a warning.

Why was it whenever she received a warning during sleep she always felt exhausted upon waking? With eyes red as if strained and complexion a pasty white she needed to take time to recover her customary appearance. Most of all she needed coffee!

An hour and half later she arrived at the office everyone there ahead of her but none looking like they had shared her nightmare. "Everyone sleep well last night?"

The question caught their attention. Not because it was an unusual question but because they knew it meant that she had received a warning. Maddox the first to speak asked, "What happened in your nightmare?"

Buick grinned, "They're going to attack the House of Commons."

Frobisher, the newest member of the team said, "We are talking about a dream not intelligence, right?"

"We're talking about one of the Boss's dreams," Dukes corrected. "Which makes it intelligence. Did you get a date and time, Boss?"

"Prime Minister Question time which means it's a Wednesday."

"Seven days away," Hughes said. "I didn't realise you were gifted with premonition abilities?"

"They're too erratic to call a gift. I seem to receive warnings of impending doom out of the blue. There's no consistency, but at least I'm able to recognise them when they find me."

"I'm pretty sure it must be hard for you?" He said eyes studying her closely.

Hughes had shown himself perceptive to the frailties of colleagues and, always ready and willing to offer support. It was his nature perhaps because of his size he had possibly grown-up helping others weaker than him. "Yes it is, but I'm tougher than I look."

"You wanted me to search for signs of spikes in homeless dead," Maddox interrupted. "I figured I'd begin with the entire map of London including suburbs before reaching out beyond. Your nightmare may have revealed something significant. Two large spikes occurred during the past week around Lambeth and Westminster."

"I don't believe in coincidence," Buick replied. "The use of both areas might be just what we're looking for. Identify where the largest proportion of homeless deaths occur in both Boroughs and the nearest cemeteries to them. They won't want to travel far for food."

"Already done," she said. Laying a map of both Boroughs across her desk. Penned circles highlighting where the highest volume of deaths occurred together with the nearest cemeteries to the high death rates. “Streatham Cemetery on Garret Lane Tooting and Brompton Cemetery,” she said pointing at the map.

“We need to visit both,” Buick said. “Billy you and Toni take Brompton. Helen and I will take Streatham.”

“Me!” Frobisher exclaimed.

Buick turned to her, “Is that a problem?”

“No Boss, just surprised,” she said with a wide grin.

“Don’t let it go to your head. Bran has no choice but to remain at the office.” It was common for officers stuck inside to snap at the chance to get out. Frobisher in her early twenties had proved to be a bit of a rebel with some authority figures. Impetus and too willing to use her own initiative when she felt it more expedient to do so. The kind of individual Buick was always on the lookout for. Her initial approach had caught Frobisher at a low when she had just been blasted by her Inspector over an unfavourable statement that made his leadership appear poor. Her career on the edge of an abyss she had jumped at the opportunity to be reassigned.

Since the beginning of IMP Buick had often found herself searching cemeteries. Finding herself among the graves at Streatham all too familiar. Whether Frobisher felt as eager as she had earlier less certain as they moved around under a blanket of heavy rain and charcoal grey cloud with a chill wind sweeping over the landscape of headstones. It was the kind of weather befitting a horror movie grave scene, all that was missing a monster of some kind.

"What exactly are we looking for Boss?" The young, uniformed officer asked. Eager to do well in front of her boss she felt unusually nervous about making a mistake, even more so than confronting a supernatural entity.

"You'll know it when you see it," Buick said. "It will be so out of place no one can miss it."

"Are these doorways to other realities always found in cemeteries?"

"Many are, but I've come across others elsewhere. Wherever you find them they all have one common denominator, being on sacred ground. That includes ground that may have been blessed hundreds of years ago."

"What about a mausoleum like the one over there," she asked. The structure sat isolated towards the far end of the cemetery in front of tall green perimeter railings.

Buick paused to study it through the heavy rain. It would have been easy to miss almost camouflaged by overgrown bushes either side. It's poor upkeep out of place with the rest of the well-maintained cemetery. No sign of a sentry outside but that was to be expected as they would not want to draw attention. "Let's take a look."

They moved towards it shoes sinking into the sodden earth making her grateful she had slipped overshoes on to resist the mud. The suction of their movements loud enough to be heard as the mud turned to sludge which seemed to hang onto their feet as if to slow progress. By the time they reached the crypt Buick was puffed while her young companion skirted it for signs of access.

Standing close the age of the crypt was obvious. Its white stone badly weathered pitted with a crusty smear of black filled with green mould. Frobisher stood directly in front of what appeared the only access. A stone door inscribed with a short epitaph stating: 'Those without Hope welcome'.

"As bleak goes that hits the spot," Frobisher said. "I'd better go first."

"Why is that?" Buick asked recovering her breath.

"No offence intended Boss, but I've been kick boxing for the past ten years. If we need to run I can slow down anyone behind that door."

"Have you got the crucifix I gave you?" Frobisher expected a human form. If anything was behind the door she might be shocked to discover it anything but human. The initial shock of meeting your worst nightmare either caused an individual to run or freeze. In either event she would be the one to deal with it and for that reason allowed the young officer her moment.

Frobisher revealed the crucifix clasped in her right hand. "And I'll recite the Lord's prayer."

"Okay, but be careful we don't know what might be waiting. These things are usually fast"

The door did not possess a lock and as Frobisher pushed her weight against it a groan from its hinges and scraping of its base against the stone floor announced her intention over the heavy rain. Slowly, gradually it moved inwards with the pressure until striking the inside of the crypt. With the door open the dull grey afternoon light proved inadequate to brighten the pitch-black interior.

"Is that what you expected?" Frobisher asked. "A black hole?"

"Maybe I should go in first," she replied.

"No sweat Boss, I should do this," the young woman said and stepped into the darkness searching a pocket for her mobile and flicking on its dazzling light.

The immediate appearance of an Illegra caught in its beam amplifying the shock. Its ungainly shape lacking a definable outline was a huge dark mass of constant movement while the resemblance of thin arms and legs provided something familiar. Yellow circles that glowed with an odd luminosity resembled eyes but on a face that was constantly moving between torso neck and head. Frobisher would have been forgiven had she frozen or turned and run away instead she swung quickly kicking it in the head or at least where its eyes were. The Illegra staggered back more surprised than injured.

Beside her Buick began reciting the Lord's prayer while the crucifix in her right hand glowed as she raised it up. The prayer growing in strength as she stepped forward. The entity wailed staggering back its features too contorted to easily distinguish. That it was in pain enough for them to keep moving forward their crucifixes raised as their words found its target.

The sudden emergence of a blue glow on the rear most stone appeared abruptly as if someone had thrown a switch.

"The access to our reality," Buick said. "Keep going we must force it to return."

Even a momentary delay in her prayer gave the creature strength. It paused arms raised as if shielding from an invisible enemy before lashing at them. Its talons moving with such speed they felt the rush of air lick their skin as the deadly nails missed. Louder than before Buick recited the prayer making the Illegra scream loudly. Staggering it turned and half fell into the splash of blue on the wall and disappeared.

"Is it over?" Frobisher asked.

"Not quite. Quickly we must smash the stone." Buick removed a hallowed blade from the satchel still hanging over her right shoulder. Estimating the centre of the stone she stabbed it with all her might. A thousand cracks ran in every direction before the entire wall fell to pieces. The weather immediately whooshing in spattering them with wind and rain.

"It would be nice for the weather to brighten up," Frobisher said.

"One down one to go I guess," Buick said grateful that she had brought her newest recruit along. Most people would have been daunted coming face to face with an Illegra, but

Frobisher had taken it in her stride. She even landed a kick on it. She was tougher than she looked which could only be a good thing. The supernatural often dealt quickly with those overwhelmed by its terrifying appearance.

***

Hughes and Dukes entered the Brompton cemetery through a narrow gate at the south entrance at roughly the same time as Buick reached Streatham. The rain was heavy, clouds were darkening while chilling blasts of wind increased in ferocity.

"Do you want to split up?" Dukes asked. The weather was doing absolutely nothing for her appearance even wearing a waterproof hood. The damp was getting through turning her hair curly and unmanageable. "We could do this quicker if we did?"

"Sorry Toni, but I'm not letting you out of my sight. These monsters could snatch either of us without the other knowing. Better we stay together. Time doesn't matter."

"Okay," she said slightly disappointed. Appearance was everything to Dukes. Not that she ever appeared as anything other than beautiful with a long list of admirers to confirm her popularity. For her it was simply that she wanted to appear as presentable as possible every minute of the day. Besides, she had learned that her appearance counted when doing her job most effectively. Her personal motto: *stun 'em to grill 'em,* had grown out of her using appearance advantageously. Some called her vain, but she figured they were blind only seeing surface gloss rather than the successful results. Of course, she enjoyed being admired as well. Comforting herself with the fact that her fleece had a hood fastened under the chin limiting the damp was she decided the best she could do in the circumstances.

"Let's follow the perimeter all the way round," he suggested taking the lead. She followed staring at each of the graves they passed searching for the presence of an entrance to another reality. Whatever that looked like? After a while her conclusion was it wasn't as easy as she had first thought. Not knowing what to look for was a handicap but Hughes wasn't deterred. Before Frobisher he had been the new boy on the block and also someone who refused point blank to believe in the supernatural. That was until he went one to one with a demon who almost snapped his head from his shoulders. An incident that was a game changer. These days he was out to make sure that nothing from other realities remained long enough to do serious harm.

They were still moving between a line of end graves and green railings when he stopped. "Look at that."

Dukes peered through the heavy rain at a grave twenty feet in the distance. A bluish glow emanating from its headstone. “Is that a reflection of the storm above us?”

“Not that I can tell,” he replied. “Let’s take a closer look.” Moving between the graves they wound their way to the odd coloured headstone. A growing sense of danger began to tease his senses making him momentarily pause to look around.

“Do you think this is what we’re looking for?”

A blue candescent light circulated from the centre of the headstone emanating heat that touched their faces making the rain turn warm with steam the closer they got.

“Buick said anything out of the ordinary.” He said returning his attention to the stone.

They didn’t hear or see the hooded woman until she was almost on top of them. Hughes glanced in her direction just in time to see her racing towards him with a blade raised high in her right hand. But it was Dukes who acted, throwing herself in front of the big man grabbing the woman's right wrist as she did and twisting it backwards. Her momentum enough to temporarily halt the danger as the two clawed at one another with their free hands. The woman grabbed the string under Dukes chin and pulled. The knot gave easily, and the hood flapped away leaving the Sergeant's hair to fall free soaking up the heavy rain.

Dukes snarled like a tigress and punched the woman so hard on the nose it shattered bone. Undeterred the woman grabbed her long flowing hair wrenching her head back hard exposing her throat. Dukes wriggled and twisted with such ferocity a clump of hair at the side of her scalp got pulled out before she freed herself. Her attacker swung back with a blow that caught her under the chin and threw to the ground.

Hughes squared up throwing a punch that contacted the face under the hood. Hitting it hard enough for the hood to fall open revealing a sharp featured female with jet black hair. The blade still firmly in her right hand. He pulled out his own blade and they circled one another like a pair of wild animals looking for an opportunity to strike.

"It's Dang's wife," he said as Dukes clambered to her feet, blood running down her cheek from a bald patch at the side of her head.

"Put down the knife," he said.

Her smile was nothing short of wicked as her eyes narrowed to blackened slits of evil. At a run she slashed at his stomach slicing open his coat down to his shirt. Dukes dived for her legs stabbing at her thighs with her own blade. Its pointed tip digging deep into a muscle. She screamed. A shrill unearthly sound that resonated across the cemetery. Moments later she dropped onto a knee. Face pained. Expression defiant. Blade ready.

Dukes had rolled away quickly rising to her feet. Her blade jammed in the woman's thigh leaving her with only the crucifix for defence.

Under the heavy rain the earth turned to mud as Hughes spotted more figures moving silently towards them. Half a dozen hooded women with blades in their hands coming to join the fight. "We've got to get out of here!" Dukes backed towards the gate. "Get the motor running, I'll be right with you." At the gate he stopped and turned to face their pursuers. In the distance two were helping their wounded comrade while others spread further apart moved silently towards him.

Dukes hit the horn several times as he exchanged blows with the leading female. Her hood dropping back revealing angular features and jet-black hair before his blade cut her cheek. A sudden mist of steam burst into the wet air as a smear of black blood ran down her cheek. Hesitating as another joined her Hughes raced away diving in through an open door beside Dukes. The vehicle's front wheels spun in protest as they escaped.

Hughes straightened himself on the seat and called Buick on his mobile. "What do you want us to do Boss?"

"Return to the office. Father O'Malley will meet us there."

"Are you okay?" Dukes asked as he pocketed the mobile.

"Yeah, but that was close. Those things are damn fast even as humans."

"You think they're Illegras?"

"I do since they all look the same," he said. "The last one I cut was the spitting image of Mrs Dang. Guess they can only take on a single form. Handy for us."

***

Father O'Malley sat in Buick's office briefcase on lap as he reached in and pulled out half a dozen new blades placing them alongside one another on her desk. The different colours of each handle catching Buick's attention. These were new something she had never encountered.

"In this world," O'Malley began. "You will regularly discover something fresh. These blades have not been needed for almost fifteen hundred years since the last time the Illegra were here."

"Why do we need them this time?" She asked. "We dispensed with one group without too much trouble. The other might be a little more difficult but we'll visit them in force next time."

"The Illegras have a hierarchy and we cannot take unnecessary risks. The oldest will prove more difficult to destroy. Age makes them stronger unlike humans."

"What are you not telling me?" She had begun to recognise a few of

O'Malley's 'tells', like the way he offered only part of an explanation.

"We have reason to believe some of the Illegra currently in our reality are the same who came fifteen hundred years ago. That means you need these blades to destroy them."

"How do you know this?"

"The Church has its ways," he smiled reaching into the briefcase again. "This is only for you. It will magnify your harmonics tenfold. Wear it always as a broach. Never take it off even when you go to bed. It will also warn you when danger is close."

"This investigation is looking more serious by the day. Should I be concerned that we may not be able to contain it?"

"No one knows," he replied sympathetically. "We do what we can and hope it is enough. That's all any of us can do."

"How will we know which of the Illegra to strike from the coloured handles?" She asked lifting a golden handled blade from the others.

"The blade glows white when you're within a few feet of its mark."

"Must we really wait until it's almost on top of us?"

"For the moment these are the best I can offer. I've already asked Rome for additional help."

"What does that mean?"

"A group of specialist priests will be visiting the UK. Should you ever find yourselves likely to be overwhelmed contact me and they will find you."

She sensed O'Malley was still holding back. Sensed an unfamiliar nervousness from his body language that indicated his concern was greater than usual. Yet he was clearly not about to share his reservations. Not at this time. To her unexpected news that a group of priests were travelling to the UK only acted to agitate her own fears. Whatever was happening at a supernatural level was big and together with her nightmare warranted attention.

They were interrupted by Hughes, “Are we intending to return to the cemetery because if we are we should leave now before they move the portal?”

“Come in,” Buick said, the big man followed closely by Dukes stepped into her office.

Father O’Malley rose from his seat, “I will leave you with your new gifts Superintendent, unless you have further use of me?”

“We might have some questions only you can answer,” Hughes said towering over him.

“In which case I am happy to help,” he smiled up at the big detective and returned to the seat keeping the briefcase on his lap. “How may I be of help?”

Buick remained silent allowing Hughes to lead the conversation while Dukes leaned against an outer office partition. The missing clump of hair very noticeable.

"We've just come from Brompton cemetery where we stumbled onto a bunch of Illegras protecting a portal."

"The Superintendent informed me," O'Malley said. "You hope to return to destroy it?"

"That's right, but Toni and I figured because it's a headstone they can probably take it someplace else. Are we right?"

"Yes," he replied. "But not in the way you're thinking. They do not need to physically move the headstone they were using to move the portal. From their reality they can close it and reopen it anywhere else they choose. That, I imagine is what they have already done."

Discovering that a rival had an edge was never an uplifting experience but less so when it came to the supernatural. Humans were very much the underdog something no one in IMP underestimated. Hughes had recently come to terms with the fact that being a powerful physical human meant little against supernatural entities. Not that it prevented him from putting himself between his colleagues and aggressive supernatural beings whenever the opportunity arose.

"So, our returning to Brompton is pointless?" he said.

"Yes, they have already moved the portal elsewhere." O'Malley leaned back on the seat and appeared to be considering its new location.

"Will it likely be far from Brompton?" Dukes asked.

"We understand they wish to attack your government," O'Malley said. "It is a very unusual strategy for creatures who prefer to stay in the shadows. We always try to figure out their ultimate goal and from what we know happening in other countries it may be they have decided the time is right to make themselves known to the entire world."

"You mean this is also happening overseas?" Dukes asked.

"Indeed," he replied. "To date in forty-one other countries all in the West. Perhaps Satan himself is about to make an appearance. I haven't seen anything like this in my lifetime."

"Do you believe in God Father?" Hughes asked.

Some questions are asked to provoke an angry response from those who clearly represent what they are being questioned on. Not O'Malley. He appreciated from experience questions about God and the reasons why others might devalue his faith when confronted by seemingly impossible odds. In a soft friendly tone he replied, "I believe God is in all of us. I believe that we cannot simplify God to one individual who oversees what we do or what we are. God is an infinite number of souls united and speaking with one voice. The reason demons and devils come after our souls is because they are the energy of life. They're indestructible and will energise whoever hosts them hence we are all at risk. However, when a demon is killed all its captured souls return to God the unified soul and thereby empowers God with the goodness needed to maintain our balance with evil."

Hughes was uncertain what to think. Certainly O'Malley's answer did not match what he expected. Schooling in religious knowledge had always leaned towards a single powerful individual as the creator unlike O'Malley's collection of unified souls speaking with one voice. "Are you saying that our God more or less disassembles himself to provide each human with a part of him?"

"Genesis one twenty-seven Then God said, "*Let Us make man in Our image, after Our likeness, to rule over the fish of the sea and the birds of the air, over the livestock, and over all the earth itself and every creature that crawls upon it.*" Notice he uses the term '*Let **us** make man in our image*'. I believe he is referring to when his unified form with our souls are as one. That he is capable of generating infinite parts of himself to be carried by each of us on a world teeming with humanity reveals his support for us as well as an ability to monitor what we do and need."

"So, why doesn't he play a more active part by destroying evil immediately it rears its head here?"

"Are you telling me that he isn't doing that through us or that by using us as his tools that he isn't allowing us to learn to fend for ourselves?"

Hughes fell silent. Buick never interrupted such conversations because she found it personally worthwhile hearing and learning the perspective taken by the clergy. However, time was short, and she needed to find where the portal had been moved. "Is there any other help you can offer us in finding where they've taken the portal?"

"I wish I could," O'Malley said.

"Then we'll start by returning to the Dang's. The wife is clearly an Illegra and therefore likely to know. We need to capture her."

O'Malley gestured a halt with a hand, "If I may Superintendent. A confrontation will inevitably lead to either your officers being injured or worse or the Illegra dying. It is too important that we know what it knows. Much better to watch and wait."

"You think we should keep her under surveillance?" She said. Her only hesitation down to the time they had before Wednesday came around. Monitoring Mrs Dang meant tying up two officers in the hope they were led to the portal. Meanwhile the rest of the team needed to find an alternative and at that moment she couldn't think of any. Investigations were never straightforward and required painstaking research to discover clues. The Internet was useful to a point but no replacement for seeing and meeting people for themselves.

"I think any attempt to capture an Illegra is fraught with danger and unlikely to produce the desired result for us," he replied.

Buick noted the '*us*'. It was good to know that he saw them united. Occasionally in the past she had been less certain their goals matched. The Church appearing to possess its own agenda, but not this time. Her phone rang a temporary distraction as she raised it to her ear, "Superintendent Buick."

"Hi Betty, it's Frank." Marshal sounded troubled. "I'd like us to meet up later. Say for dinner. Call it work and pleasure. The Italian in Stratton Ground. Eight?"

"Sounds good, is everything alright?" A tinge of excitement raced through her veins. Marshal had a nice voice she thought.

"My apologies, it's been a hectic kind of day," pausing momentarily as if gathering his thoughts before continuing. “We found a few things that you might be able to explain better than most given your role.”

“If I may be of any help certainly,” she said. “See you there.”

Looking up from her desk when finished she found an audience of three silently watching her. Hughes took the opportunity to breach the silence, “Is everything alright Boss?”

Someone must have heard her earlier conversation with Marshal and guessed the reason for his call. It was a small office and the Boss being courted was bound to attract interest. Though she was less certain that was all that was on his mind after hearing the concern in his voice. Hoping her complexion did not change she met their gazes with a neutral expression, “Yes, I’ll be meeting with Marshal this evening. Something sounds as if it’s got him rattled.”

“You think he ran into an Illegra?”

She guessed that wasn't it otherwise he would have kept her on the phone longer. No one could encounter a supernatural entity and suppress the numerous question that came from such a meeting. "Maybe, but I don't think so. He was looking into the big guy outside the Dang's place. I'd guess it has more to do with him."

"Well, if you're finished with me for now Superintendent, I'll be on my way," O'Malley said rising from the seat. "Should I hear anything about the portal I'll let you know."

Curious she thought. How could he learn the location of the portal? The temptation to ask never reaching her lips before he departed.

CHAPTER FOUR

The Italian restaurant was small and sparsely occupied. Marshal had arrived ahead of her sitting right at the back facing towards the door with his back to the wall. Smiling as she entered rising up from the seat to greet her and helping her slip out of her wet raincoat which he handed to a waiter. She kept a scarlet scarf around her neck and straightened her blue jacket before sitting down. Her satchel lowered gently to the floor beside her chair. Their eyes made contact the way two people interested in one another do as the waiter took her order for coffee.

"You sounded concerned over the phone?" She said.

"We almost cornered your guy. He changed hotels for a small one along the Vauxhall Bridge Road. An anonymous tip warned us."

"Anonymous?" She repeated.

"A woman. High pitched voice with a foreign accent possibly East European," he said. "Anyway, he must have seen us coming and escaped out the back." Taking a moment before continuing his gaze never leaving her own. "This guy might be good, but he made a mistake leaving a notepad."

She sipped a glass of water before asking, "That sounds useful but who do you think made the call?

"Impossible to know. Not a friend I guess."

"At least we know he's human, leaving the notepad was a human mistake."

"It supplied us a thumb print and we've been able to identify him. His name is Mario Conti. American Italian forty and a hitman for an organised crime syndicate in the US. To date he's managed to escape prison five times at court for separate murders. Needless to say the Yanks would like us to grab him in the act." He took a sip of water before his expression darkened. "We also found another list which included those on the first but with a few extra names."

"And these additional names are what's troubling you?"

"Jonathon Suffolk Tory MP for Ridgewater."

She frowned highlighting creases around her eyes that he momentarily admired. "Terrorism?"

"I was hoping you might be able to help me with that," withdrawing his mobile he showed her an image from Conti's pad. "Have you ever seen this before?"

The sketch of a sword standing erect on top of a hill with the Sun sinking down on the horizon behind it. The sky half black half blue. Her expression revealed it was familiar. "This is the symbol of the Magna Earth Cult. In Latin Magna means Great. As far as I'm aware we haven't heard from them for a couple of years. They're more visible and vocal on the North American continent."

"Do you know if this Cult is involved in organised crime?"

"I've never had a reason to research them to any real degree, but imagine it very possible."

"How did you come to learn about them?" His tone suddenly firm inquiring.

"A couple of years ago one of their leaders visited a nest of mystics in Islington. We were investigating them in regards child trafficking. Half a dozen kids had gone missing hence we were invited to participate in the investigation. However, the cult woman who visited didn't remain long enough or indicate any reason for us to follow up on her after leaving."

He smiled apologetically, "Sorry, I just realised that I'm quizzing you."

She shrugged, "I'm not offended. We're on the same side. Now it's your turn. What are you not telling me?"

His momentary surprise quickly disappeared, “You’re as sharp as I figured. Okay, there’s a note about one of your officers. Bran Maddox. Her name is circled in red on the back page of his little book. What connection does Maddox have with any of this?”

Bran Maddox was a very good officer and friend. Having repeatedly demonstrated her loyalties over the past few years. The notion that she was somehow involved with any part of this investigation other than officially not something Buick was willing to believe. “Whatever the reason I refuse to believe it’s because she’s in anyway involved.”

“If I were you I’d feel the same about one of my officers, but we need to find out why Conti has her mentioned in his pad. I was hoping you would ask her. If there’s a simple explanation we both need to know.”

She gave him the benefit of the doubt because he didn’t know Maddox and being angry at him for doing his job was unreasonable. Besides, he still had nice eyes and was giving her the kind of look that she hadn't seen in a long time. "After we eat we can drop by the office. Maddox is sleeping there until further notice."

"She is?" His confusion was predictable and so she decided to explain and watch his reaction. "What I'm about to tell you is classified. The reason I'm telling you is because eventually you're going to come up against the enemy my team regularly struggle with. When you do you need to be aware what's confronting you."

"All this because Maddox is sleeping at the office?" He said.

"She was touched by a creature from another reality. An Illegra. Now they're able to find her wherever she goes hence she remains at the office until we resolve whatever's going on. We don't want them knowing where our investigation is taking us."

His expression changed. Not to anything bad or repulsive but his gaze no longer stared into her eyes as if attempting to see her soul. Now they appeared to be asking themselves a question about her sanity. A smile suddenly broke through all the confusion, "Okay, I don't think you're kidding but you have to admit it's pretty wild."

"Return to the office with me after we've finished eating."

"You still want to eat?" He said.

"We're in a restaurant and I'm hungry," she said. "You're paying by the way. Because you think one of my team might be rogue."

"Okay, but what if it turns out Maddox is rogue?"

"She's not!"

"Maybe, but what if she is?"

"Then I'll reimburse you," she said. "Now can we order."

***

Maddox was sleeping in the accommodation next door to the IMP office. Mirrors and all reflective materials had been removed leaving a dull matte finish to avoid the emergence of any supernatural beings. Since the talon had appeared from her mobile and touched her hand the idea another might appear had never been far from her thoughts. The prospect of being face to face with an Illegra horrifying yet also fascinating in some weird grizzly way. As she slept her mind became aware of a presence something heavy climbing on top of her. Invisible. Its presence in her dream wrapping her in a cocoon that divided her from reality. Its hands reaching for her throat. Gradually encircling her neck with long bony fingers that possessed a vice like grip. Asleep Maddox hands reached for the invisible monster throttling her. The weight pressing down on her growing heavier by the second as her head twisted from side-to-side eyes closed.

The hands around her throat strong resistant to her attempts to be free. Uncertain how or what placed the words in her head. She found herself being asked for the location of Philip Dang. An odd question and one she didn't know. The creature seemed to sense her inability to help and suddenly backed off. Coughing, gagging she awoke only to discover the burden on top of her real. Its hands round her throat. Real. She couldn't see it but there was no doubt it was there. Was she about to die. Murdered by an invisible killer from another reality.

What prompted her to begin the Lord's prayer a mystery, but that's what she did even though it might be the last words she ever uttered. The creature's reaction immediate. Its grip relaxing its weight rising from her.

"Bran," Buick called from the corridor outside.

The door swung open, and the corridor light flooded into the small room with its single bed. The dark shape of something not of this world captured momentarily as it rushed out brushing passed her and Marshal. Knocking them aside so easily they banged hard against a wall before catching themselves from falling.

Marshal stared after the creature, "What the hell was that?" It appeared transparent features indistinguishable as it ran and disappeared into a wall.

"An Illegra," Buick told him rushing into the room to check her colleague.

"I'm okay," Maddox said sitting up and turning her legs over the side of the bed placing both feet on the floor. "How did it get in here?"

"Father O'Malley told me what I needed to do if one ever did," Buick told her. "This will protect us from further attacks at the office." Rising to her feet she began reciting words in Latin moving out of the room into the hall then into the outer office before moving into her own. Marshal joined Maddox staring down at her uncertainly. Oddly lost for words. Joining her on the bed he sat beside her for several minutes before finding something to say.

"If I hadn't seen and felt it I might never have believed it."

"You won't be the first," she said rubbing at the purple-coloured marks around her throat.

"It was transparent or at least that's how it appeared as it brushed passed," he added.

"Did it touch your skin?" Maddox asked.

He shook his head, "No, I don't think so."

Buick returned moments later, "I should have done that earlier. My bad. How are you feeling?"

The other woman sighed, "Strange. As if I should know something that I've forgotten."

"I'll make us some coffee. Let's go next door." Sitting down at the desks in the outer office coffee mugs steaming beside them Buick asked, “What do you remember?”

Maddox wearing a dressing gown over her blue coloured onesie studied the air as if trying to recall all that happened. “I was sleeping when I felt this weight on top of me. I thought it was part of my dream.”

“What were you dreaming about can you remember?”

“I think I was trying out some clothes in front of a tall mirror, something like that.” She stopped and looked at Buick. “Can they come to us through our dreams?”

“To be honest I don’t know but what other way is there down here?”

“That’s seriously scary,” she said. “I don’t know that I’ll ever be able to sleep again.” Maddox had been able to compartmentalise the supernatural creatures she encountered to date because there had always been separate from her reality. The idea that a dream allowed them to be conjured into her reality changed everything. It was as if they were a constant almost a part of her.

"You'll be alright now that I've carried out the shielding ceremony. They cannot appear anywhere in here."

Hearing that and accepting it were two different things she thought. Perhaps Buick was mentally stronger than she could ever be?

"Hold on guys, I'm playing catchup here. Are you claiming that thing whatever it was arrived here via a dream?" Marshal asked still coming to terms with the existence of supernatural beings. The thing that crashed past him in the corridor and dived into a solid wall proof enough the women were neither exaggerating the supernatural nor bordering on insanity. As the kind of man who always figured he had both feet firmly on the ground this latest piece of information required time to digest.

"It appears that way Frank, "Buick said. "Until we know otherwise we have to believe it did."

"But that means everyone is vulnerable," he said raising Maddox gaze and confirming what she was already thinking.

"Welcome to our world," she smiled turning back to Maddox. "The big man I spotted outside the Dang's is a known hitman called Conti. Frank's crew almost had him, but he got lucky and escaped." She waited until certain Maddox understood. A blankness in her eyes indicated she was reliving her dream and the invasion of the room in which she had been sleeping. Buick gently squeezed her hand to bring her back from wherever her mind was taking her. The pressure worked as Maddox turned her gaze in her direction focusing on the Superintendent. "He left behind a notepad with your name in it circled in red ink. Do you have any idea how he'd even heard of you?"

The other woman looked at her. Eyes puzzled bottom lip trembling, "No."

"Are you alright Bran, do you want me to call a doctor?" She had come across enough trauma victims to recognise the signs Maddox displayed. Right now she needed to know she was safe that help was at hand. She benefitted from having a disciplined mind one that had regularly experienced the unimaginable and so far coped very well.

"No, I don't want to sleep again, and they're bound to give me a sedative. I just need to get my head round what happened. I can still feel its weight pressing down on me and its hands round my throat." With that she burst into a flood of tears cupping her face with both hands and sobbed. The tears helped as if allowing her fears to be drained away.

Taking Marshal aside Buick said, "She's in no state to answer questions at this point. I need to call someone who might be able to help her."

"I understand," he sympathised. "Also, I'm really sorry things turned out like this. I was hoping we'd get to know one another better..."

"I don't think we've done so badly, especially after you saw what you did. Give me time and I'll find out if Bran knows why her name showed up in the notepad. However, I have a theory if you'd like to hear it?"

"Always," he said.

"Conti is a hit man who might be responsible for killing several accountants. Arthur Burns is last on the list, but we now know that Philip Dang is also an accountant which cannot be an accident. Also, that Dang's wife is an Illegra and Burn's wife a high priestess at the Satanic Chapel."

"Okay, but where are you headed with this?"

"It appears that Conti is the enemy of both Burns and the Dangs.

Which means he's also an enemy of the Illegra. Bran was touched by an Illegra and is now acting as a beacon for them showing her whereabouts which might have exposed our whereabouts too. Hence they knew she was here and probably the reason I'd ordered her to remain while the rest of my team investigate. What I'm wondering is whether Conti somehow found out about Bran and may consider using her as well."

"You mean to locate Dang?"

Buick frowned, "I wasn't thinking that but why are you?"

"We took Dang into custody; sorry I hadn't mentioned it before. It's obvious he knows more than he's willing to share and while we're missing two detectives I'm prepared to make him sweat. He's safely hidden for the moment. If Conti thought IMP might be given access to him it makes sense that he'd track Maddox to Dang's hideout. But how would a hitman know about any of this supernatural stuff?"

"Because he's not just any hitman. The Magna Earth Cult sent him, and they do know about supernatural stuff. There's no knowing what artefacts they gave him to complete his task. What we might have stumbled into is a supernatural war between two human factions, the Satanic Chapel, and Magna Earth Cult."

Marshal felt his head spin. The leaps his imagination had been asked to take enormous even for the most grounded individual. "Can you tell me if Dang is human?"

"He is as far as we know. Billy Hughes can usually identify supernatural entities."

Marshal nodded everything made sense in a skewered sort of way. "As for Arthur Burns I have his home under surveillance and uniformed officers in a vehicle outside back and front. If Conti goes anywhere near we'll know." He paused long enough to catch his breath. "Where do you think Jonathon Suffolk Tory MP for Ridgewater fits in?"

She shrugged, "It won't be the first time a politician was found involved in the dark arts," she said. "I can do some research to find out if he has any links to either of our two rivals. What do you want me to do if he has?"

"I've so far kept this low profile. I wanted to be certain we had something concrete to take to management. Hence I wanted to discuss it with you before talking to my boss."

"And now?"

"I'll talk to her in the morning and say what we're doing," he paused thinking about his next words before speaking. "If you find him associated with either of these supernatural groups leave me to pass that on to my boss. I'd prefer that she decide whether or not to include your Commander Brandown. I got the impression that he's a stickler for rules and at this moment in time I really can't see how any rules apply with what we're dealing with. At least my boss Chief Super Carrie Hobbs is likely to be flexible given the situation."

He had recognized Brandown's limited capacity to handle issues outside the norm without even meeting him. It was an astute observation. One she liked. "That's fine just let me know what's decided. At some stage we might need the anti-terrorist people to get involved."

"Agreed. As for your theory it makes sense and I'm willing to bow to your knowledge of both our supernatural enemies as well as your colleagues. I won't pursue Maddox but do keep me up to speed with what happens with her. Is it possible she's possessed, that thing with the dream is really creepy."

"She's definitely not possessed trust me on that."

After Marshal had gone she called Hughes explained what happened to Maddox but didn't have to ask him to return to the office. He was climbing out of bed as they spoke. Next she called a psychiatrist friend named Jocelyn Cornish repeated what she had explained to Hughes and this time asked her to attend the office. An hour later both were with them. Cornish used Buick's office to discuss what happened to Maddox while Buick and Hughes sat in the outer office discussing what they needed to do.

"Do you think Bran's in danger?"

Buick shook her head, "Not for now, but I'm worried that if she ever leaves here we might not be able to protect her. We need to solve this. The sooner the better."

"What about this Conti character?"

"I think he might want to use her as bait."

"I thought you told Marshal that he wanted her to find Dang?"

She nodded, "At this point it's an obvious option. However, supernatural beings don't do anything without a reason, and I suspect whatever they want from Bran is more complicated. Conti somehow knows what that is I'm sure of it. There's no other reason he would have her name."

"You want us to find him ahead of Marshal?"

Hughes had worked with her long enough to guess how her mind worked. "We don't have a choice. If I told Marshal he'd have done everything he could to stop me. I'm still not sure that he completely trusts me yet."

"Give him a chance," he said. "He just discovered the truth about the supernatural. That's a pretty big leap for any ordinary copper."

"I know," she agreed with the expression of someone who had

survived to tell the tale. “The world is a confusing place when you add other realities. Trouble is we haven’t time to nurture him. Our task is fairly straightforward. Find Conti to discover what he knows about Bran.”

“What about this Tory MP Suffolk?”

“No idea at this point. Just another reason we need Conti.” She rose from the seat, “As soon as Jocelyn’s finished we all need to get as much rest as possible. In the morning I’ll get Helen and Toni to carry out all the searches on Suffolk.”

“What about Conti?”

“If I’m right he’ll be on his way here.”

“Here!” Hughes exclaimed.

“He’s working on behalf of the Magna Earth Cult. They’ll ensure he somehow gets through building security. He’ll try taking Bran from us. We need to be sure we disappoint him.”

"Is it possible that he'll be able to do things?"

She grinned; Hughes still found it difficult discussing the supernatural. "They're bound to have given him artefacts that might be able to affect us and help him."

"What does that mean for us?"

"Well he's human so I imagine that means his actions will be limited by his mortal body. Meaning that we don't need to worry about him reaching us through dreams like the Illegra."

"And we can capture him if he does come," Hughes said trying to sound positive.

It was eight in the morning when Frobisher arrived and woke Buick who was sleeping on the chair behind her desk. Four hours sleep more than she had expected but not nearly as much as she needed. "Why does your mouth always feel like an armpit first thing in the morning when you haven't slept well."

Frobisher appeared a little stunned by the question, “Maybe a longer sleep is needed to get rid of that feeling?”

It was a weak effort to comfort her Boss, but it’s the thought that counts and considering the hour not a bad effort. Buick nodded, “Let the others rest especially Bran she had a rough night.”

“Yes Boss,” she said turning to leave the room. “Helen I want you and Toni to search the names of the individuals in the emails I sent you. I need all the information on them that’s available. I’m particularly interested in the MP and his known associations with any supernatural group.”

When alone she closed her eyes and rested while considering all events to date. She always found that playing with specific features of an investigation in the morning could provide fresh ideas. Significantly they had discovered something that the Illegra possessed the ability to reach humans through their dreams. Unsurprisingly no living human was aware of this ability since they hadn't been to Earth in fifteen hundred years. What that might mean for IMP and its team nothing good. They would likely all now be targeted by the creatures what that meant for each of their mental attitudes only time would tell, but she needed to do something calm fears to a minimum otherwise no one would get any sleep.

The report on the death of Arthur Burns first wife appeared fairly straightforward. A motoring accident followed by his meeting Emily, a High priestess of the Satanic Chapel. It could not have happened without a reason she thought. The Satanists wanted Burns on their side for a reason, but what that was still eluded her. For a moment she wondered if the same were true of the Dangs. An image of their lovemaking fleetingly flaunted itself in her mind. An Illegra and human the picture grotesque made her eyes snap open. Nasty! Not wanting a repeat the image she kept her eyes open while running through what else she knew.

Currently the MP Suffolk had a large question mark over his head. An MP's involvement possibly indicating a connection to her dream. Why Conti had his name threw up dozens of possibilities all bad. As she toyed with more ideas a wave of weariness swept over her. Struggling to remain awake proved futile as the warm office embraced and comforted her in the chair. Without realising she again slipped into asleep. A couple of hours later Dukes woke her.

"My goodness, why'd you let me sleep?"

"Because you obviously needed it and we've been busy," Dukes replied hands on hips clearly ready to argue.

"Well I hope you have something for me," she said noticing Duke's change in appearance. "What's with the hair?"

Dukes grinned, “You noticed.”

“You changed the side you part your hair, it’s fairly obvious to anyone who regularly sees you.”

She lifted the hair covering the right side of her scalp to reveal a large bald patch. Several small cuts clearly visible. “I couldn’t walk around with that on view.”

“You bled,” Buick noted. “Did it cut you with its nails?”

“I don’t think so. It was more to do with the way it yanked my hair out. It’s okay I feel okay.”

“Just don’t do a Billy on me. If you start noticing anything I need to know immediately.” She said unwilling to let any of them suffer alone being tormented as a result of supernatural changes. She needed to discuss what was needed with the psychiatrist Jocelyn Cornish and made a mental note to do just that for the entire team.

“Sure thing. You’ll be glad to know we found something,” her expression changed as she dropped a wad of papers on her desk. “Suffolk turned out to be very interesting for several reasons.”

Buick stared down at the paperwork then looked back up, “Make it easy for me Toni. Sit down and tell me in what ways has he proved interesting?”

She did as asked and sat on the seat opposite, “Three years ago he visited the US and apart from meeting government counterparts he spent time with Victor Agar the head of the Magna Earth Cult. Since then they have met another half dozen times. Also, Agar is associated with Vladimir Turgenev a Russian industrialist.” She paused a hint of more excitement bubbling inside. “Through a contact I have I was able to discover that three years ago Suffolk was estimated to be worth around one and a half million pounds. Today his net worth is around thirty million.”

Buick had already guessed the likely identity of Dukes contact a sister working in the banking system who appeared to be helpful on the odd occasion she needed information. Bending rules was sadly becoming the norm to do their job properly a reflection of authority baulking the investigative process to hide what was happening at a senior level. Not that she had as yet shared any of her concerns about management corruption with her team. Creating unrest among them served no purpose as she needed them focused on the job in hand. Also, they were clever enough to be able to put the pieces together for themselves starting with Brandown.

"We need to bring Marshal in on this. He can sort out the MP while we deal with the supernatural."

"What about Burns or Dang?"

"Dang's wife told us she was from Berlin. Our contacts at Interpol are checking her out. Do you think it's possible for an Illegra to remain in our reality indefinitely?"

"Father O'Malley seemed clear that's not a good option for them. However, we discovered something he didn't know, that they can reach us through our dreams. That and the fact they haven't visited our reality in fifteen hundred years makes me wonder if he was simply attempting to put our fears to rest over the time they spend here. He does that sometimes when it suits him. She recalled an incident in which O'Malley claimed a demon did not possess the power to resist the Lord's prayer until one did. Apparently demons have a hierarchy the higher up they were the stronger and more resistant to Earthly defences.

"Do you like Father O'Malley?" She asked.

"Like him," she repeated thinking over her relationship with the priest. It had been odd from the outset with him appearing as if from nowhere while she confronted a demon intent on decapitating her. Saving her life and apparently her soul had begun the foundation of their relationship. Oddly, however, O'Malley was never someone to spend time discussing life in general. He arrived abruptly and left the same way. There was never time for her to gauge whether she liked or loathed him. He had grown to be a necessity. A useful contact. "To be honest I don't know how I feel about O'Malley. We've known each other over several years and I'm still uncertain."

"I'm not sure this means anything," Dukes continued. "Arthur Burns medical record shows that since his wife's death he's been seeing a psychiatrist."

"I'm not even going to ask how you know that." Buick said.

"Doctor Desmond Hope's clinic is located in Harley Street. His charges are astronomical yet Burns meets with him every couple of weeks. My point is that he's out of Burns league. It's impossible to believe he can afford this guy."

"Maybe he's a client of Burns and they've done a deal?"

"I'll double check, but we ran off a list of his and Dang's clients and don't recall seeing Hope mentioned. I've got Helen doing a background check on Hope." Brandown 's entrance made Dukes rise from the seat, "I'll let you know what we find."

"How are you getting on with the missing detectives investigation?" His brusque question made her sense something had him agitated. His entire demeanour came across as tense and hostile.

"Marshal wanted us to check out the supernatural aspects of the investigation which is what we're doing."

"Did you specifically mention IMP is concerned with the supernatural to him?" Brandown made it sound as if to do so was bad.

"Yes," she replied. There was little point hiding it. The rules that applied allowed her to do so at her discretion.

"Do you think that was wise?" He asked moving up and down her small office hands behind his back as if unable to relax. The more she saw of Brandown the less she liked. He was a stickler for rules and regulations without much thought about how they applied to situations that did not specifically cater to their requirements. IMP needed a leadership that understood rules were superfluous when dealing with the supernatural. Brandown was not that kind of leader.

"It was necessary," she said. "It's becoming clear that both the Satanic Chapel and Magna Earth Cult are involved. We believe as rivals. The Cult sent a hitman to the UK to apparently kill off accountants either employed or members of the Chapel."

"So I was informed by Chief Superintendent Hobbs, Marshal's boss." Buick said nothing as his gaze fixed on her as his striding paused. "I thought I'd hear about your case from you before anyone else, I mean you do work for me don't you?" It was intentionally snide sounding. Brandown wanted her to know he was in charge and that any friends she might have above him would take his word before they listened to her.

She continued in a neutral tone, "Marshal wanted to pass it by his boss first to get an idea what she thought about what we'd learned. He asked me to wait until that happened before I informed you. Is something wrong Commander?"

He glowered. "In future I want to hear from you first not someone else. I don't ask much from those of your rank, but respect is something I expect from day one."

She nodded. The urge to state that respect was earned not freely given just because someone was of a higher rank caught on the tip of her tongue. With great resistance she did not voice her feelings. "I did not intentionally mean to show you disrespect. I apologise if that's the way you feel."

"Maybe, but you did, and I do!" Brandown kept his hands behind his back their reflection in the glass partition behind him revealed they were tightly clasped. Not a good look for any superior who wanted the respect of a subordinate. Being angry because she merely used the discretion allowed her was acceptable under the rules, even for him. Also, a suspicion that he was intentionally attempting to keep IMP from proving itself useful kept repeating itself to her. Something she would not allow without a fight.

"May I ask you a personal question Commander?"

His gaze thawed slightly, "Yes."

"Do you believe in the Devil?"

It was an unexpected question and not one he considered relevant. With an expression bordering on scorn he said, “What do my beliefs have to do with your investigation?”

“All our investigations are in some way associated with religion. I think it matters that our senior manager is open minded when we begin an investigation that identifies supernatural entities.”

“What I care to believe or not is absolutely none of your business Superintendent. We both have jobs to do and mine is to ensure that you abide by the rule of law.”

“You do appreciate that in regards the supernatural there are no man-made laws,” she replied.

“But they still apply to any human contact you having dealings with, that’s what I’m most concerned about. What you do with anything else you claim to encounter is up to you provided you do not place any of the officers under you in danger. Does that answer your question?”

“Not in the slightest,” she said. How a senior officer with access to all the files relating to IMP investigations could still doubt what she and her officers claimed to have encountered merely reflected his own personal limitations. Brandown did not want to believe in the supernatural. In fact she guessed he was intent on doing whatever he could to deny the presence of supernatural beings. His reason never a question people like him were ever challenged to answer. "I don't need you to be an obstacle when what we do is tough enough already!"

He ignored her, "What happened to Maddox?" She felt the blood rushing to her head subside before her anger got the better of her. "You've got her living here and she was seen by a psychiatrist. Why is that?"

"She was attacked last night by a supernatural entity called an Illegra. One of these creatures had previously made physical contact with her and by doing so made her act like a beacon for them. We can't risk including her outside this building with any aspect of the investigation otherwise they'll know what we're doing. Fortunately, the way the Illegra got in has now been blocked."

"Did anyone else see this Illegra?"

"I did and so did Marshal."

"Why didn't you tell me that he'd seen the thing?"

"I just did," she said.

"Don't be flippant with me Superintendent!" He snapped eyes blazing. "From this moment on I want regular feedback from you on this investigation. I mean every hour. I always want to be informed immediately one of your officers is injured in any way."

Buick's anger was bubbling same as Brandown only the fact that others were watching made her suppress it. "I give you warning I may need to go over your head for permission to continue as I always do."

"Do that and you'll make an enemy who never forgives or forgets. Your choice," he said before leaving her alone the others in the outer office watching after him.

"That looked fairly intense," Maddox said from the door.

"He's taking time acclimatizing to what we do," Buick replied as she picked up her mobile and called a friend at the Cabinet Office. Maddox moved away closing the door behind her as Buick explained the difficulties Brandown was putting her through and the need for her to act freely against the current supernatural threat. Her mention of a possible attack against the House of Commons received obvious attention that resulted in confirmation of Brandown being ordered to leave IMP alone. All that she wanted. However she guessed it would be unlikely that the Commander would be easily warned off. He had made a personal threat against her and would no doubt respond in some way. She simply hoped it would happen after the current threat had been handled.

Maddox returned eyeing her cautiously. Uncertain from her distant expression whether she was ready to discuss what she had been able to discover about Dr Desmond Hope. "I've info about the psychiatrist treating Burns."

"Come and sit down."

"Are you okay?" She asked having witnessed and angry scene from the outer office.

"Dealing with people who refuse to even try to understand what we're doing makes life difficult, but nothing I can't handle. What have you got?"

"Desmond Hope's real identity is Davit Arman. Parents were Armenian. His surname means hope so I guess that's where he got the idea for his English name. He's been in the UK for twenty-five years. Qualifications originated in Russia, and he had to undergo a re-registration process that took five years before he was allowed to work in the UK."

"How was he funded while studying in the UK?"

"He worked nights as a singer," she said with Buick expressing genuine surprise. "Apparently he had a good voice if the reviews are to be believed."

"Armenian," Buick said. "Another Russian connection. They keep popping up."

"What does it mean?"

She shook her head, "Not sure, but we can't ignore the connection with Marshal's investigation. Nor that the Russians could have plans about taking over the UK. Since the war in Ukraine and Putin's obvious unhappiness with us he has every reason to do us some harm."

"Some might say they've already bought enough politicians to do that. Since the war we're seeing more and more revelations about Russian money and influence at the heart of government. I'm willing to admit I'm unsure what to believe these days."

Buick did not immediately reply. Her own fears about government corruption and influence by foreign agents seemingly confirmed by journalists over many weeks. What it meant for ordinary people without proper leadership difficult to know. The country was in a mess very possibly by design and what was happening on the supernatural front could not help. Should her dream about an attack on the House of Commons be real she needed to ensure that IMP at least did whatever it could to prevent it from happening or, prevent it from being successful. "We need to be careful."

Maddox studied her momentarily. It was unusual for Buick to sound so fearfully cautious. "You're genuinely worried."

"I am. This is looking more and more like some kind of coup and not simply rivalry between two cult groups.

How it all fits together I don't know, but my instincts tell me it does. Nothing we've witnessed is irrelevant they're connected, and we need to discover how."

"Is the Commander on side?"

"He's a non-believer in what we do. He's read everything there is to read about IMP and still refuses to accept that any of us hasn't been tricked in some way."

"Shame when demons die their bodies get spirited away," she replied. "We could really use a demon corpse round about now."

Buick nodded while considering the possibility of capturing an Illegra in human form. Mrs Dang would make an excellent example to parade in front of Brandown. The problem however was that any Illegra in human form faced with public exposure would likely return to its natural state and kill all those around or die in the attempt. After which it would disappear in a puff of smoke. “I wonder what might happen if we tasered one?”

“An Illegra?” Maddox queried.

Nodding, she rose from her seat behind the desk and moved to a metal cabinet with a Manifoil combination lock. Spinning the dial right and left four times the lock clicked open. Turning a metal handle she pulled open its door. Inside sat several pieces of hardware. Between a pair of Glock 17’s she picked out a taser X26E standard police issue. Capable of delivering 50,000 electric volts in rapid pulses over five seconds. “In their human form they might be susceptible to human vulnerabilities. It’s guess work but worth a try. If we could knock one out and sit it down in front of Brandown even if it changes form in front of him and escapes he won’t be able to deny its existence.”

Maddox grinned, “It’s worth a shot.” It was the first time since her experience with the Illegra materialising from a dream that she had smiled. “Maybe we should all carry a taser just in case the opportunity presents itself. If I’d had one the other night we might already have our example.”

Buick reached into the cabinet and drew out two more, “Hand these to Billy and Toni. I want them to check out Dr Hope.”

She took the weapons and a record book for them to sign. “About Toni, I’m concerned one of those things pulled out a clump of her hair. It doesn’t make sense that she isn’t altered in some way considering physical contact was made.”

“Do you think she’s hiding anything from us?”

She shook her head, “Physical contact with anything from the supernatural always results in us gaining an ability to fight them which seems pretty odd, but it’s fact.”

“Okay, well keep an eye on her we can’t afford anyone going rogue.”

Maddox returned to the outer office dishing out the weapons while issuing Buick's instructions to call on Dr Hope.

As Dukes and Hughes headed along the basement corridor towards an underground carpark Hughes buttoned up his raincoat. "Parting your hair on the left looks good on you."

Dukes always liked to hear positive comments about her appearance. The left parting had been forced on her to cover up the bald patch left by the Illegra, and she remained undecided whether it diluted her good looks or not. "Thanks Billy. I'm still undecided."

Hughes chuckled. No offence Toni but you're good-looking whichever side you choose to part your hair. "Ah, you're a sweetie." With that she realised that she had forgotten her mobile on her desk. "You keep going, I'll meet you at the car. I need to go back for my phone."

As she approached the office door she saw that it was ajar. Irregularity is something that heightens a professional's alertness. All members of IMP were especially observant for the unusual no matter where they discovered it. Slowing her stride and muffling the sound of her footsteps she reached the door as quietly as a mouse. Leaning a shoulder to move the door gently inwards she heard an unfamiliar deep barrelled tone with an American accent.

"Which one of you is Maddox?"

Silence.

"I already figured that it's not the uniform," the voice said. "That's leaves you two broads." The sound of someone inhaling sharply made her push the door further in. A large, tall man stood in the centre of the outer office gun in hand pointed at Frobisher. "She dies unless Maddox steps forward."

"I'm Maddox," Buick said emerging from her office. "What do you want?"

"Shut up!" He snarled. "Get your coat you're coming for a ride."

"And if I don't?"

The silencer on his weapon spat smoke as a bullet buried itself in Frobisher's shoulder. "Next one is in her head."

Frobisher screamed clutching her shoulder as she spun off the seat to the floor. Buick wide eyed took a step towards her before the gunman gestured she stop. "Not gonna tell you again. Get your coat!"

Dukes fired the taser from ten feet away and hit the gunman square on the back. His bulk suddenly shook uncontrollably as the electricity flowed through him. Even so he didn't go down, turning to see who it was his own weapon attempting to line up on her. Maddox hit the back of his head with a metal paperweight that thwacked loudly against his skull. His gun flew across the office as he dropped to his knees and Maddox struck him a second time. With eyes rolling up to the ceiling he dropped forward on his face. Unmoving but still breathing.

Buick snatched up his gun before joining Maddox and Dukes with Frobisher. The uniformed officer lay flat on her back as her white blouse turned crimson where the blood poured from her wound. Fifteen minutes later she was on her way by ambulance to St. Thomas's hospital accompanied by Maddox.

In the outer office Hughes had returned while a paramedic treated the wound on the back of the gunman's skull. The expression on Hughes face after learning what had happened enough for Buick not to leave him alone with the American. Hughes was huge just a little smaller than the American and right then she doubted the American's chances of not taking a beating if they were left alone. The

Inspector's face an explosive red expressed the kind of anger a father might have for an injured daughter.

"Nothing on him except some cash and this telephone number," Dukes said handing Buick both.

"I think we can guess who he is," she said. "How he managed to get in here something else again."

As Dukes nodded something happened. She sensed it more than experienced it as some sort of physical reaction. Her vision blurred momentarily as she stared at Buick. When it cleared Buick stood surrounded by a golden aura. The Superintendent noticed the way she was staring. Confusion in her expression.

"What happened?" She asked.

Silence as Dukes looked round. First Hughes. His body glowing with a golden aura too. Then the big American on the chair in front of her. No aura. Nothing. Ordinary. What was happening she wondered? Buick stared at her knowingly. "I think something just changed."

"I noticed," Buick said. When a change occurred most were not expecting it. In this instance Dukes knew that a change was possible, but as we all do we deny the possibility for as long as we are able. Her confusion expressed in her beauty made plain what Buick had known as did Maddox. Following her into the small office Dukes sat on a chair.

"What have you got?"

Dukes shuddered involuntarily, "It's a little spooky. I'm looking at you and see you surrounded by a golden aura. Billy too."

"What about the American?"

"Nothing. What does it mean?"

"Check your hands," Buick told her.

She peered down at her hands and aura surrounding them, "What the hell does it mean?"

"You can have my working theory for what it's worth, but it's just that, a theory."

"You're theories are usually worth hearing," she replied a frown creasing her usually flawless brow. It wasn't everyday people began glowing in front of your eyes. Not as far as she knew and feeling uncomfortable about it seemed right.

"You're seeing those able to confront evil. I think whenever we're touched by something from another reality we receive a gift. Something that gives us a weapon to fight back. You can now recognise the good guys while Billy recognises the bad."

"I don't really see how recognising the good guys can help," she said. "I know who we are already. I don't need to see any of us glowing."

"Except I'm pretty sure there are more good guys out there that we don't know about. That's where you could play a significant role."

They were suddenly interrupted by Brandown and a sheepish looking Marshal. The atmosphere of the room changed immediately. Electrically charged and unfriendly. "I want your prisoner turned over to Marshal," Brandown said firmly. His expression a look of satisfaction. Denying what he knew she wanted most at that time a personal achievement.

Dukes began to rise from her seat, but he gestured her to remain. Typical of his type Buick thought. He wanted an audience to watch him win. Brandown was a nob she thought. If proof were needed this was it.

"We haven't had time to interview him," she replied. "Conti could prove crucial to the entire investigation but needs to be handled properly."

"Let Marshal get on with the interviews he is lead officer on this investigation after all," he replied leaning against the open door to her office. Ready to deflect any arguments. He wanted this win. No he needed it.

A man of his word she thought. He warned her he would make a bad enemy and appeared intent on proving his claim, even though her ally at the Cabinet Office had already warned him off. No doubt they would be interested to learn he had ignored their warning, but that would take time something they were fast using up. Petty skirmishes between colleagues was a huge waste of time but Brandown appeared happy to continue.

"I'd be happy to have you and your team present during our interview," Marshal interjected already annoyed that he had been ordered to join Brandown. Quickly realising that the Commander was intent on humiliating Buick because of his dislike for IMP and what it represented. He had learned that much on their way down to the basement. Marshal had twice attempted to explain what had occurred the other night when they unexpectedly arrived back at the office and disturbed an Illegra. Brandown refused to accept his claim suggesting the two of them had likely had too much to drink. Suggesting such a thing did nothing to win over Marshal but for the moment he was content to remain silent until an opportunity that allowed him to resolve their differences in Buick's favour presented itself. Quickly adding, "You know more about those who employ him than us."

"Would that be fine with you Commander?" Buick inquired.

"If you really think them useful," he replied to Marshal turning his back on Buick without deigning to include her in the conversation. "Do keep me informed of any progress." With that he left them alone.

"Sorry for that," Buick said.

"Nothing to be sorry about Betty. The man's an arse. He and I would have fallen out long before now."

Dukes finally rose from her seat, “Do you still want me and Billy to interview Dr Hope?”

She glanced into the outer office at Marshal’s detectives standing in front of Conti. “No reason to remain here for now. See what you can find out. I’ll go with Superintendent Marshal to interview Conti upstairs and meet you back here.”

CHAPTER FIVE

It was normal for someone who had recently discovered a new ability to be apprehensive. Much the same way the captain of a ship sails into uncharted waters not knowing what to expect. However, as he drove them to the psychiatrist practice in Harley Street with the vehicle stationery at a stop light she suddenly sat upright in the seat. Eyes wide mouth open as if wanting to speak.

"What's wrong?" He asked.

"Can you see them?" She asked nodding in the direction directly ahead of them.

Apart from a steady stream of traffic moving from left to right he saw nothing out of the ordinary. "What is it you want me to see?"

"The couple right in front of us," she said pushing herself back in the seat.

He looked again, but saw no people in front of them. Had he not been a member of IMP he would likely have ignored her and thought she was having a breakdown. "Describe them to me."

"They're both naked," she said. "But colourless and without legs. It's like they're sitting on a dark cloud."

"And you can see them directly in front of us?" He checked.

"Yes. Two black and white people. It's like they were just sketched. There's no colour to them nothing."

"How old are they?"

"Sixties or seventies I think. They staring back at me. I think they're as surprised at me seeing them as I am."

The stop light changed to green and a car behind sounded its horn. Hughes touched the accelerator and their car moved forward. Dukes eyes closed as they drove through the couple without a sound. After they crossed the junction she turned on the seat to look back, but the couple were gone. She swivelled on the seat to face the front and shook her head.

"Maybe I'm going mad?"

He chuckled, "If you are then we're both headed for the asylum. This job has a way of making you think you're seeing things that can't exist when in fact, they do. If you saw a black and white naked couple then I believe you."

"You don't have to say that Billy." She replied uncertainly.

"I know I don't, but our reality is a lot different to all the people outside this car and if we don't believe in each other who the hell are we going to believe in?"

With a sigh she reached out and touched his arm, "Thanks. It's just that I'm finding it hard believing what I just saw."

"We'll discuss it with Buick when we get back, maybe she'll have an idea what's going on."

They found a car space close to the clinic a four-storey white terraced affair with black painted window ledges and guttering. It was the kind of place easy to imagine enjoyed by rich Victorians with an upstairs downstairs mentality. The reception was larger than expected with an open plan hall and front room no longer separated by a dividing wall. Inside was painted white too with modern grey furniture and wall paintings of foreign landscapes. A thick pile blue carpet underfoot sank beneath their every step so they might have floated to the desk.

Apart from a male receptionist the reception was empty. Hughes made the introductions, and they were asked to wait until Hope had finished with a patient. About five minutes later a white-haired old lady stepped out of the nearest door with a little dog clutched tightly against her chest. Passing them a suspicious look before leaving through the exit. A moment behind her Dr Hope stepped out. A tall lean individual with jet-black hair dressed in a brown well fitted suit white shirt and gold tie. A narrow moustache below his nose. Around the mid-fifties he possessed the bearing of someone confident in themselves. A cultured voice that possessed a hint of foreign origins the only feature that distinguished him from English aristocracy. Leading them into a large office which included a chaise lounge for patients to use while psychiatrists sat out of sight behind them. The idea a gem of Sigmund Freud a famous Austrian neurologist and founder of psychoanalysis. Hope used a seat behind a large mahogany desk occupied by paperwork and laptop. As he sat down he couldn't help but notice the odd look Dukes gave him. As if witnessing something unexpected.

"Is everything alright detective?" He asked. A frown creasing his otherwise smooth swarthy complexion.

Hughes shot her a glance catching sight of the way her eyes remained wide open. He didn't understand what was going on and began the conversation. "We're here about one of your patients doctor, an Arthur Burns."

"Arthur," Hope repeated dragging his attention away from Dukes. "I'm afraid as you're aware I cannot discuss any of my patients due to confidentiality. However, can you tell me why you're interested in him. I ask because if he needs help I'll gladly offer it."

"He's a witness to an investigation relating to a pair of missing detectives."

"I see," he replied thoughtfully. "I really wish I could help you but…."

"You've been touched by a supernatural entity," Dukes blurted catching both men by surprise. "He's glowing same as us Billy."

The doctor fell silent hesitating momentarily before asking, "You see my aura?"

"Gold, just like us." She told him. "How'd it happen?"

Leaning forward elbows on the desk he grew a half smile his expression of unconcealed excitement definitely unexpected. "I cannot believe to have finally come across others who share the same bond."

Hughes found it impossible not to interrupt, "Bond, that's an odd term to use. You think us connected in some way?"

"You don't know," he replied leaning back momentarily before replacing his elbows on the desk. "Whoever challenges supernatural entities and survives are automatically bonded. We help each other without limitation."

Hope sounded sincere and Dukes wanted to know more, "When were you in contact with them?"

"It happened a long time ago when I lived in another country."

"Armenia?" Hughes asked.

"You've done your homework," he replied and rose from the desk turning towards a large window behind him to stare at the world while continuing their conversation. "We were forced to leave our home. Moscow doesn't like any in their population who challenge their authority. Before the fall of the Soviet Union in ninety-one our parents decided we needed to get out. Sadly, they were both murdered by the Russians before they could join us. My two brothers and sister reached France and remained there for ten years before I and my sister Mariam, came to England. My brothers remain in France. We fight the supernatural in both countries supporting each other when necessary."

"Why?" Dukes asked. "I mean you escaped Moscow and settled in countries that aren't oppressive. Why would you continue to fight the supernatural rather than live in peace?"

"You think we can live knowing what we do and do nothing to stop it?" He shook his head. "We knew that would never be possible. We had to do something, anything to avenge the loss of our parents." Turning away from the window he continued, "They were taken by the same beasts who tried to capture us. Moscow has its own portal to their reality and uses it to communicate and ask for help."

"You mean the war in the Ukraine is part of some diabolical plot thought up by Putin?"

"Partly, our understanding by intelligence received from one of our brothers who is an undercover cop in Paris. Is that Putin made a deal with the Devil himself to become world leader. Over the past decade his agents infiltrated the British government at the highest level. We believe some of the Cabinet are actually supernatural entities hosted in human bodies."

"I can believe that" Dukes said. "Given the cold way they treated initial pandemic victims."

Hughes shifted uneasily. It was one thing accepting that a supernatural reality existed quite another that entities from it were walking around as Members of Parliament. "Tell us when you came across a supernatural being that made physical contact with you?"

"This is going to sound strange," he started without turning back to them.

"We get a lot of that," Hughes remarked. Still uncertain what could be stranger than supernatural MPs!

"The Russians have been using supernatural entities for a long time. Somehow their scientists were able to create a portal to another Dimension and negotiate an alliance. Our parents suspected it and for that reason were singled out for termination. It happened while the four us were getting out of Yerevan the Armenian capital. We were to escape in a van driven by a family friend when we were attacked by a demon. It tore through the metal side of the van like it was paper. It claws catching all of us as it did."

"What saved you?"

"Our family friend was a priest Father O'Malley. We don't know what he did, but he got out and faced up to the creature. I recall peering out of a tear in the side and saw it disappear in a puff of smoke."

Dukes and Hughes stared at each other as if doubtful he could possibly be talking about the same Father O'Malley who had recently visited them at the Yard. Yet with only momentary hesitation she asked, "Could you describe this priest?"

"I'll never forget him," Hope said and returned to his seat. His description a perfect fit for the Father O'Malley they knew. "Why do you ask?"

"It doesn't matter," she said. "How old would you think he was at the time?"

"Difficult to know fifty possibly maybe a few years older."

Their escape from Armenia had occurred thirty years ago which meant that Father O'Malley was now in his eighties. Yet did not look anywhere near that age. Dukes sighed life was ever complicated she thought. "Can you help us with Arthur Burns?"

"Of course," he said without hesitation any restraint cast aside because of their common bond. "He's been my patient for several years. I can understand how he may be involved in the supernatural."

"No offence doctor but how can someone like Burns afford your services?"

"His wife pays. Apparently she inherited money and is able to pay. That's as much as I know."

"What's wrong with Arthur?" Dukes asked.

"He suffers with what I term Mirrored Memory." He saw from their expressions a complete lack of understanding. "He appears to replace his own memories with those of another."

"Is that like schizophrenia?

"No. It's a form of psychosis in which the patient loses sight of reality rather than occupying two or more personalities. Arthur always knows who he is. He never speaks as though he were someone else. What he does is talk about memories as if they were his own but that clearly belong to someone else. Usually children no more than ten years old."

"Are these memories from someone he knows or strangers?"

"A bit of both, I think," he said. "The real problem is they take up space in his memories where he should be recalling things that occurred to him at an identical time. Yet his personal memories covering the same period remain lost."

"How is that possible?" Hughes asked.

"I wish I knew," Hope replied. "I suspect the supernatural is involved for a couple of reasons." Leaning back on the seat he appeared to search for the right words. "Are you aware that his present wife is a member of the Satanic Chapel?"

Hughes nodded.

"She is a very high-level priestess and over time I've become concerned that she might have somehow been involved in the death of his first wife, Julia."

"What makes you think that?"

"Julia was a nurse working at a local hospital. His second wife Emily joined the same hospital a few weeks before her death and very quickly became friends with Julia. Arthur met her on more than one occasion before Julia was killed."

"And?" Hughes asked not yet seeing any connection.

"The truck that took out Julia's car was owned by the company that had previously employed Emily. A haulage firm called Burrows Hauliers Limited."

"Coincidence," Hughes added.

"The company claimed the truck had been stolen. The thief responsible for the crash was never found. There were no witnesses, so it appeared a straightforward hit and run."

"Yet you still have issues, why?" Hughes asked.

"Did you know that Emily, his second wife has an HGV licence. She was actually employed by the Haulage company as a spare driver as well as an admin clerk."

"You think Emily rammed Julia's car," Dukes said. "Then escaped on foot?"

"I look at scenarios much the same way the police do, searching for something that appears unusual."

"That's a bit of a leap doc," Hughes said.

"Perhaps, but sometimes you have to go with your gut," he grinned.

"What makes Arthur Burns so important?" Dukes asked.

"About four years ago he was hired as a sub-contractor to handle the accounts of a company called Zero Trek. To cut a long story short I discovered from Arthur that it's a company owned by a Russian oligarch. Vova Stepanov a close associate of Vladimir Putin."

"The Russians seem to be around every corner," Dukes added.

"Putin is a very dangerous man who initially wants to reassemble the former Soviet Union, hence the Ukraine war. He then intends to expand Russian influence across the whole of Europe if not militarily certainly through the use of supernatural entities able to replace the top tier of governments with creatures that will follow his lead. He has been very successful over the past decade creating doubt and suspicion between members of the European Union. The UK is an example of what Russian propaganda has been able to achieve. Brexit hit the Europeans hard but not as badly as it did the UK and continues to do so. The British people have been duped into believing they would be better off out of the EU. In fact the opposite is true but only now are some beginning to realise it. I suspect Arthur knows something that threatens Vova Stepanov but instead of killing him they continue to use him. I imagine his wife being from the Chapel increases his usefulness as he handles accounts for several arms manufacturers here in the UK. While he cannot recall what happens whenever he works for them, apart from what he has recorded in ledgers he cannot be considered a threat to their operation."

"Is this all supposition or do you have credible evidence?"

"When you were touched by a supernatural entity you were given an ability to identify people like yourself," he said to Dukes. "With me it's as if I can walk around their heads to discover what makes them tick."

"So, you've no credible evidence," Hughes said. "This is just another going with your gut exercises."

"You know it's more than that. I'm telling you that whenever I walk around Arthur's head I find snippets of information that I have gradually pieced together which I just presented to you."

"We do understand, but you can appreciate why we have to be cautious about anything we're told," she turned her mobile towards him. "I just looked up Stepanov. He's worth around a hundred billion dollars. If we're going to tackle someone like that we can't afford to have holes in whatever we present. Currently Stepanov is not blacklisted by this government."

"Are you surprised?" Hope asked. "He will have billions invested around the UK and needs time to get them clear of the tax man."

"To be honest I am still surprised. It's fairly blatant and I wouldn't imagine they want that," Hughes said. "I thought all oligarchs were meant to be banned from the UK with more immediacy?"

"You'd be surprised how many still fly through our airspace. The government stance is that we cannot tar all Russians with the same brush as Putin, but the fact is the oligarchs are as much a part of his regime as his generals. Your government is infiltrated with a great deal of infighting going on behind the scenes."

"You told us your sister escaped to England with you, what is it she does here?"

"She works with me, also as a psychiatrist. In fact she's next door with a patient as we speak. She will be very pleased to know that we have met one another. It has been a very lonely burden for us."

"I find it hard to believe you have never come across others like us?" Dukes said.

"Not many have your ability to see us for who we are. One of my brother but he's in France most of the time. They have larger groups there because of him."

It was easy to admire others with the supernatural knowledge fighting monsters in the UK without help. They both felt it, Dukes the only one to show it while Hughes remained as impassive as ever.

"I do have a question for you doctor," Dukes said. "Have you ever heard of black and white naked people who don't appear to have any legs floating around on a dark mist?"

He nodded, "You can see them also, that's amazing."

"Who are they?"

"We think they're spirits who have not ascended to another plain of existence. Somehow they're trapped in our reality but what the reason might be no one knows."

"Has anyone been able to communicate with them?"

"Not as far as I'm aware. Can you?"

"I have no idea, but they know I saw them and looked straight at me."

It was a lot to take in for Hughes, but he was getting better at it. Turning to Hope he asked, "What ability does your sister possess?"

"She can see through the eyes of others," he answered and recognised their confusion. Leaning back against the window he added, "Imagine if you were able to see through the eyes of someone you spotted two blocks away who was facing towards a hidden corner. You would know who and what lay ahead of you before you arrived."

"Cool," Dukes said.

"Does she need to know the other person, or can she simply use them?"

"She has two choices," he said. "The first is that they must be in line of sight. Using her ability in such a way allows her to use anyone."

"And the second?" Hughes wanted to know.

"Mariam can make physical contact with someone and connect with them anywhere and at any time in a twenty-mile radius."

"Wow," Dukes replied clearly impressed.

"Has she used this on patients?" Hughes asked quickly appreciating the freedom such an ability allowed to spy on patients.

"She has, but only in extreme cases where we have been unable to help a patient. She tried her ability on Arthur Burns but failed to see anything. We have assessed her ability to be effective on ninety percent of the people she meets. Sadly Arthur was not one."

"What happened with Burns?" Dukes asked.

"When she tried she was met by a black impenetrable wall of energy that bounced her attempt back to her body. I recall how shaken she was the first time, but it didn't stop her making two or three more attempts until she finally had to give up."

"Do you have any idea what this impenetrable energy is?"

He shook his head, "No, but Arthur is not alone being shielded by it. As I say we assess that at least ten percent of the people she has met also have it."

"I would like you and your sister to meet our Boss," Hughes said. "I'm sure you will both get on and there may be much to share likely to help us both." He handed Hope a business card. "Just let us know when you'd like to visit."

He read the card and noted the address, "I will discuss this with Mariam and contact you soon."

***

The interview room they inserted Conti was occupied by a desk three chairs and recorder. The seat Conti occupied loudly complained each time he shifted on it as Marshal and another detective sat opposite. Marshal noting the time and occupants after pressing the record button.

Behind a mirrored screen Buick sat alone watching them. The big man could be key to discovering what was going on but whether he would be willing to talk something she felt less certain about. No doubt Magna Earth used him because he was reliable and unlikely to easily hand over information about them or why he was here.

"You shot a police officer," Marshal started. "Not the brightest thing to do considering where you were at the time."

"You people are out of your depth," Conti chuckled. "You have no idea what's coming."

"Why don't you tell us?" He replied.

"That would spoil the surprise," he laughed.

"You're not going anywhere until you do. You might as well get accustomed to living in a cell for the next thirty years or so."

"Do you really think I'd break into a place like this without a back-up plan?"

Buick leaned forward on her seat putting her face closer to the glass separating them.

"A back-up plan, is that right." Marshal said.

The big American smiled without humour as he crunched something between his teeth. Within seconds his body shook uncontrollably before his head fell forward with a thud against the table.

Marshal jumped to his feet and checked for a pulse in the American's neck looking at the two-way mirror as he did so. "He's dead."

CHAPTER SIX

With everyone meeting back at the office including Maddox who brought news about Frobisher being stable after surgery removed a bullet from her shoulder. Her family were with her and would keep the team updated. Buick welcomed news about Dr Hope and his sister which added a fresh supply of people capable of helping them. However, the most tantalising news was about Father O'Malley and how his age. She had always felt O'Malley was keeping things from her but the latest revelation from Hope suggested something unnatural behind his presence.

Yet she remained hesitant over bringing the Hopes and O'Malley together, something both Dukes and Hughes urged her to do. Their argument that they needed to be certain O'Malley was truly on the right side of the supernatural threat and that secrets were commonly considered necessary in order to deceive. Why O'Malley never mentioned his past or the pivotal role he played on behalf of the Church left many questions unanswered. The possibility that he had helped them in the past to fulfil some hidden agenda of his own remained a distinct possibility, but whether it also worked to their detriment she found hard to believe. Yet after Maddox supported the other detectives Buick allowed herself to be swayed. Arrangements were then made for the Hopes and O'Malley to attend together and thereby reveal whether he were one and the same as the priest from thirty years ago.

The following day the Hopes arrived together a full hour ahead of O'Malley. Mariam Hope in her early fifties was plump around five feet four inches tall and well-groomed in a blue trouser suit under a light tan raincoat. With long jet-black hair that defied her age she appeared ten years younger at first sight, but the closer she got the more lines around her dark eyes revealed the passing of time. Like her brother she spoke excellent English with an accent that was distinctive if not immediately recognisable. They were led into Buick's office and offered seats opposite the Superintendent while Dukes brought them coffee in paper cups. The detective sergeant feeling a little embarrassed that they had no decent porcelain to offer guests. A pattern of behaviour associated with the way she always wanted to appear as presentable as possible.

"Paper cups are fine," Mariam Hope said with a warm smile.

"I'm not going to beat about the bush," Buick began. "We wanted you here to meet the Father O'Malley we've been dealing with over the past few years. I'm told that your description of the one who assisted you thirty years ago sounds a lot like the same individual we know."

"You think they're the same." Desmond Hope frowned recalling the image of the priest who helped them escape so long ago. Without grasping that Buick was confounded by the possibility he had not aged. "He would be in his eighties today. It would be good to see him again we have so much to thank him for."

"I didn't want to discuss this over the phone, but there's something you should know before he arrives." She could feel their attention focus. "If O'Malley is the same person you remember he remains between forty-five and fifty-five in appearance." She waited for her words to sink in. Their expressions naturally reflected as much confusion as she felt. "I can imagine what you're thinking, but since dealing with the supernatural I've come to learn that anything's possible. If true why O'Malley hasn't shared his ageless appearance needs to be understood by us if we're to continue trusting him."

He leaned forward placing the coffee cup on her desk, “You’re suggesting that Father O’Malley is some kind of supernatural entity himself. If that were true his actions to date surely shows he’s on the side of good.”

She shrugged, “We cannot accept that without some kind of explanation. Gaining our trust has provided him access to investigations that would ordinarily have been forbidden. It also allowed him to in some instances steer an investigation in the direction he chose because of information he provided. Clearly, if he is the same person you remember it presents us both with reason to want to know much more about him. How did your parents come to know him?”

“He was our local priest moving into the area when we were children. What are you intending to do Superintendent should we identify him as the same person we knew all those years ago?”

“Well as far as we can tell he’s on our side so nothing that would change that. I and my team would like an explanation. I’ll let him clarify what we suspect and if everyone’s happy we’ll continue as before.”

“Have you ever asked him about his past?” Mariam Hope asked.

“Never had the chance. He rarely stays long enough other than to dish out weapons and recommend what we do. I think the only time he’s remained longer was the other day when Billy asked him questions about God. At first I thought he might be upset but he seemed content to be as helpful as he could.”

“I must admit I’m curious now,” Mariam said. “After all these years we never encountered him here even though he’s obviously operating in London. I can’t believe he was unaware of our presence.”

“Mmmh,” Buick murmured. “You think he’s aware of your presence but has avoided contact?”

"I think Father O'Malley is a very resourceful man who has always known much more than he is ever willing to share. For me from the age of ten until he helped us escape his answers to my questions were often ambiguous. Direct responses were never his thing he made me imagine what he might mean rather than spell it out. I'm sorry that's not very clear either, but do you understand what I mean?"

"Yes," she replied. "He's an enigma."

O'Malley arrived on time. The IMP team together with the Hopes sat in a semi-circle in the outer office. After a uniformed officer escorted him to the office he removed his light mac and hung it on a door hook before joining them. His customary briefcase rested on his lap. If he noticed the presence of Desmond and Mariam Hope he did not show it as he occupied the only empty chair between Hughes and Maddox.

"We have some exciting news Father," Buick said, standing in front of the semi-circle of listeners.

"You have," he replied. "You discovered Desmond and Mariam."

While remaining seated he turned to his left, "It is good to meet you both again after so long."

The rug felt as if it had been pulled out from under Buick's feet, but she was quick to regain her balance. "We all have questions that we'd like you to answer."

"I haven't aged over the past thirty years," he replied flatly like someone expecting to hear the dinner gong and not being disappointed.

Buick was beginning to wonder if their offices were bugged by the Church. "Can you explain how such a thing is possible?"

He rose from the seat and placed the briefcase on it. "Please be seated Superintendent and I'll explain what I'm able; this meeting is long overdue and quite necessary." He waited while Buick returned to her seat. "The Roman Catholic Church has taken the lead against supernatural evil for thousands of years in and around the European continent. Other religions have done the same elsewhere around the world. It is as you can imagine a constant battle." Hughes began fidgeting like he had better things to do than hear a history lesson. O'Malley continued without being fazed. He had done this same thing dozens of times in the past. Each time a little differently to adjust for advances in technology and updated knowledge about the planet and universe. Twenty first century people had advanced well beyond those he encountered in the early twentieth century. He couldn't help being amazed by the creativity and ceaseless desire of humanity to understand its place in the universe. "There has always existed a need for consistency among the warriors against the supernatural. For that reason some of us were chosen to have our lives extended."

"How long is extended in your terms?" Hughes asked suddenly still and attentive.

"Until I am no longer needed," he replied.

"When were you born?" Dukes wanted to know.

His face creased up with an expression that suggested he was about to say something few would believe. "Five zero six A.D."

"Thirty years before the Illegra last appeared on Earth." Buick noted.

"Yes," he agreed. "Their appearance was taken as a warning that the threat they posed was incredibly destructive to our reality."

"But who decided you should live longer; it can't be the Church they don't have the power to extend life. Well not as far as I know?" She said.

"I cannot explain further," O'Malley replied. "Not because I do not want to give you the answer you seek, but simply because I do not know the answer."

"The only being who could extend your life is God," Hughes said. The big man wanted to use logic to fill in the gaps the priest kept blank. God to him seemed the likeliest answer and looking around at the others he appeared to have their agreement.

"All I am able to tell you is that before I was chosen a month of prayers led up to my selection. My apologies in advance but I must reiterate some history," he said staring directly at Hughes. The big detective nodded for him to continue expression neutral. "In the early sixth century Cardinals were a new rank introduced to the Church. Prior to that they had been referred to as "eminent" or "superior". The prayers were carried out by a group of newly introduced Cardinals over the space of a month.

Those men only paused between meals and sleep when not repeating their prayers. They even took it in turns to eat and sleep at different times in order that the prayers were incessant. We could all hear them from our quarters. Their words meaningless to us. They were chanted in an unfamiliar dialect with harmonics that now and again made the walls tremble. Also, for more than a month Rome never saw a clear blue sky. Dark, grey clouds occupied the heavens twenty-four hours a day. It was a very strange time."

"So, what exactly are you telling us?" Hughes leaned forward elbows on knees head tilted with his square chin jutting out in the priest's direction. His eyes revealing uncertainty like someone who had just been told to believe the world was flat.

O'Malley had seen the same expression again and again over the centuries. Believing the impossible or improbable was a massive leap for most and one that few could accept. Fortunately, the twenty first century had broadened the minds of humanity to accept far more than they were willing just one hundred years before. Yet, nothing he had to share could answer the question they all wanted to hear. That he had met God. That would be a lie or at least it would have been stretching the truth. After his selection he had slept for an entire month. A coma of sorts the priests around him suggested and when awake all he could recall was a bright flame and deep barrelled voice speaking to him as a father to a child. Explaining what was expected of him while stressing the necessity for secrecy. Who the deep barrelled voice belonged to was never explained in his dream although he was inclined to believe if not God than one of his angels. His other memory after waking was feeling incredibly hungry. He could have literally eaten a horse. Since then he had never had a day ill or felt physically tired. He did not need sleep but did so occasionally because it was considered normal and, after the first hundred years without sleep decided to fall into a normal routine to make himself less obvious. However, he never had further dreams or at least none that he could ever recall. Sleep became something other than a state of peace and rest and he was often annoyed with himself for taking so long to succumb to its other offerings. It was a metaphysical experience in which he travelled the other Realms to meet and debate with spirits. His discoveries always fresh in his mind upon his return to the physical reality they all dwelt. It was also from the other Realms that he obtained information about the threat posed by other Dimensions. The war with evil was not only taking place in his physical reality but on every conceivable front in every Realm. However, whether Buick and the people around him would gain anything hearing about the wars in other Realms was debateable with the possibility of clouding their growing awareness of issues in the universe with an overload of information. For that reason he felt it better to focus on what Buick and her people needed to do in the here and now. "There's nothing more I can add to help you come to terms with my age."

"Are there any others like you?"

"Yes, though I have never met any. We maintain our own regions with people like yourselves. The Church acts as a conduit through which we communicate as well as from where we receive our instructions."

Hughes had a million questions. Maybe more than any of his colleagues but one question that was arguably less important kept repeating itself in his head. "What's it like to be you?"

O'Malley guessed the big detective's meaning. "Being immortal?" Hughes nodded. "Let me make one thing clear. We are all immortal. Our spirits live on after our bodies die and decay to dust. Our spirits are made of energy which is indestructible. Therefore when our bodies die our spirits or consciousness continue by transferring to another plain of existence, another Realm."

"Okay, Hughes continued. "But you're physically bound to our reality which must be different?"

"Very," he agreed. "The honeymoon period lasts for the first hundred years. By then everyone you grew up with is dead and you have to begin establishing new long-term relationships. That appears to be instinctive to our species. By the time you reach five hundred years old you do your best not to become too fond of those around you. I know that might sound cold but losing so many friends as an immortal I find emotionally draining. After a thousand years you come to terms with the reality that spirits return. Something that oddly took me a long time to discover because I refused to sleep for so long and therefore did not acquire access to spirits who taught me what I now know."

Hughes head shot up as if he heard the dinner bell, "Explain what you mean by claiming that you refused to sleep?"

"I do not need to sleep for the same reasons you do. I do not need physical rest. That's not to say I don't feel tired but with me I tire when mentally drained not because of physical exertion or because I haven't slept in a year."

"What do you do at night?" Maddox asked.

"During the first five hundred years of immortality I often observed the stars, as what you call an astronomer. Of course the equipment available was fairly basic but I improvised and made star charts as best I could at the time and began to realise just how vast the universe is."

"And these days?" Maddox continued.

"I sleep regularly to watch over the world from the astral plane and to meet spirits to discuss matters important to me."

No one spoke. A pin hitting the floor would have sounded like a car crash. Finally Buick found some words, "Are you ever granted future insights Father. Any indication about what we should do that might prove helpful to us?"

He smiled sympathetically, no doubt again asked the same question over and over covering many centuries. "The future remains unknown to me as it appears to do for all the spirits I encounter on the astral plane."

"That's a lot to take in," she replied.

"I know," he agreed. "However, it is necessary that you understand the basics of life and death in our reality. My own perception of what occurs around us is now indelibly moulded by the different interconnected Realms of existence embraced within this one and only accessed metaphysically."

"You mean our minds," Maddox wanted confirmed and received a nod of agreement from the priest.

Turning slowly to Desmond and Mariam Hope O'Malley continued to smile. "It is truly good to meet with you again and I apologise for not having contacted you sooner in this physical reality, but know that we have often connected on both the astral and sub-terranean planes."

"Did you deliberately not meet with us here?" Desmond Hope asked.

His head tilted to one side the way dogs do as if to help them assess what was expected, "You and IMP needed to meet to defeat what lies ahead."

Hughes couldn't help himself, "Is this what is meant by fate?"

"I don't know," O'Malley shrugged. "What do you think?"

"How should I know, you're the fifteen-hundred-year-old expert?"

"It was your idea. You must have collected your thoughts from what I've told you." The priest said.

Everyone stared at Hughes not knowing where his thinking was headed. The big detective suddenly appeared uncomfortable, "Okay, okay, let me put it this way. Is there such a thing as fate?"

"If my actions are intended to make things happen then I would agree with your idea, but I'm not sure that's how it works. Sometimes things just happen spontaneously."

Buick was brooding over what O'Malley had said about IMP and the two Hopes needing each other. It indicated that O'Malley either knew something about the supernatural enemy facing them that he had not disclosed or, he was simplifying their united strength being more powerful together than as two distinct individual groups. Something which was obvious without saying it. She wasn't sure that asking him more would reveal the truth if he preferred it remain unknown to them.

"Will you stand beside us when the time comes to confront the enemy?" Mariam Hope asked.

"Perhaps," he replied turning to her. "I need to discuss doing so with Rome. However, they have already loaned you a dozen priests."

"And when can we expect to meet them?" Buick asked.

"They will join you at the appropriate hour. Before then they must remain in prayer to boost their strength."

"You seem to place a lot of value in prayer," Maddox said.

O'Malley looked at her as if she had said something so obvious it didn't need saying. Such as don't cross the road without looking left and right to check its clear. "Why wouldn't we? The most powerful weapons we have are associated with our senses. Sound and smell are two extremely potent senses. The harmonics from the Lord's prayer is a well proven defence. Many other prayers offer defence against a variety of creatures from other Dimensions." He returned to his briefcase to collect several leaves of paper. "This prayer is for each of you and one of the oldest ever written. My understanding is that it was specifically written to ward off Illegras." Passing the prayer around each who studied it before Hughes spoke.

"I can't read it Father," the big detective said. "I wouldn't even know how to begin."

"I can," Maddox said. "I haven't ever seen this language before either, but I'm able to read and understand the words."

O'Malley smiled gently before replying, "You need to study the words detective. Push any doubt aside. They want you to understand them and when you finally properly see them they will remain forever in your memory. Recite it daily and you will provide yourself with protection from the Illegras for twenty-four hours. You will not suffer any harm when the Illegra is destroyed but will become vulnerable to physical attack."

The paper Maddox was holding abruptly disappeared in a puff of smoke which startled her. "What the heck!"

"When the words know they are memorized the paper on which they were written will disappear as your one has just done." He said and looked over to Buick whose paper had also disappeared. She nodded knowingly. Moments later the other papers disappeared including that held by Hughes.

"Now that is weird," he said.

"It was Edward Bulwer-Lytton who in eighteen thirty-nine claimed that the pen was mightier than the sword. His spirit has not yet been reborn, but I do look forward to a time when we meet again."

"He was one of you?" Dukes asked.

"One of us," O'Malley corrected. "Yes, but obviously not an immortal."

Hughes might have felt that he was dominating the questions debate but nothing like that ever prevented him from speaking out. "Are you telling us that our spirits return to this physical reality?

"They do," O'Malley answered.

"And you also claim there are multiple Dimensions or Realms in which our spirits journey is that right?"

"Not in the way you describe. We refer to Realms when talking about our physical reality. They are infinite in number and we all must travel through them eventually."

"But you're immortal so you can't do that can you? We can because we die," Dukes felt an urge to clarify this latest snippet of information. Ignoring that her emotions felt as if they were being overwhelmed. The same way a child feels taking that first step into a sweet shop.

"You can trust your instincts detective," he told her. Doing so will help absorb what you are learning quicker and more comfortably.

Her jaw sagged a little at how he had known what she was feeling. What she had no appreciation of was that he had gone through this process so many times in the past and witnessed dozens of different reactions that nothing he was witnessing today had not been witnessed many times in the past.

"I remain here until I am no longer needed. Afterwards I will become like you and journey through other Realms. In this physical reality we count time differently compared with Realms. This physical reality is the shortest of journey's for our spirits because it attracts multiple lessons not found anywhere else that need to be repeated before we can be assured to comprehensively understand them.

Hence our spirits return here some more often than others because we are, even as spirits, individuals. Learning and understanding emotions ranks high among our needs. Those who choose to act against humanity do so opposing all they've been advised. The frailty of humanity in regards adhering to humane codes of practice is something that baffles our spirits. It is a hot topic of conversation when they reach other Realms."

Hughes stared blankly at O'Malley. Life had appeared so much easier to understand before their acquaintance. "Do demons and Illegras come from these Realms?"

"No," the priest replied. "They exist in different dimensions hence they are not a part of the natural order and create chaos whenever they visit. If they were ever to establish a foothold in our reality. By that I mean conquer a country to establish a base. Their first step will be to construct a mine that reaches the Earth's core.

The Earth will implode and act as a black hole taking the entire universe with it."

"How does that work?" Maddox asked.

"They will transmit energy from their dimension to the core and by doing so generate a conflict at the atomic level that will cause an implosion." He paused momentarily. There was so much that he needed to explain and so little time but at least they all appeared to be accepting what they had learned so far. "Dimensions are completely different spheres of existence hence a portal is required to journey from one to the other. Realms on the other hand, are constant and always with us even now as I tell you about them. We share this same spot-on Earth with billions upon billions of other Realms. Invisible to us due to innumerable distortions."

"You mean," Desmond Hope said. "That at this present moment

where we are is also occupied by billions of others?"

"That's precisely what I mean, both in a physical as well as a spiritual reality."

"I do not understand how it's possible?" Hughes said. "If we share the same physical area why aren't we bumping into one another?"

"I am not a scientist and therefore my explanation is only what I am able to understand. All those who share the spot I am standing on at this moment operate at different harmonies and speed and by doing so cannot interact. That said, sometimes we are able to sense another presence when there is a lapse in the field that separates us. "

"This sound more complicated than time travel," the big detective said. "I don't suppose time travel is real?"

"That depends," O'Malley said.

"On what?" Her wanted to know already considering the possibilities time travel would offer by travelling back in time to correct mistakes.

O'Malley appeared to read his thoughts, "Not in the way you mean."

"What does that mean?"

"No one fully understands, but let me explain something that current science already knows that might help," he said. "Have you all heard of Alpha Centauri?" No one replied. All had heard of it but hearing about it and actually knowing what it was other than a spot in the night sky might have been thought a little embarrassing. Without wishing to show ignorance they remained silent including Buick. O'Malley continued, "Alpha Centauri is a gravitationally bound system of the stars and exoplanets nearest our Solar System. In space terms it is a mere four point thirty-seven light-years from our Sun."

"Are you about to tell us UFOs are real?" Hughes asked not immediately recognising the direction O'Malley was taking them. As a man who always wanted facts about any specific issue he figured the priest might be attempting to big them down with science.

O'Malley ignored him, "We can see Alpha Centauri using telescopes. What we actually see is light emanating from it that has taken four point four years to reach Earth even travelling at the speed of light. Therefore what we see is light from the past not the present. Now imagine living on Alpha Centauri and looking at Earth the same would be true."

No one spoke including Hughes. Absorbing this fresh piece of information already giving him a headache.

"Different periods in our history remain visible to other worlds not simply because of distance but also due to the past in our physical reality needing to reflect itself. The fact it does means it is ever present. Think of it as a video recording that can be replayed revealing any period and you begin to understand where I'm coming from."

"No offence Father but I really don't understand what you're telling us?" Hughes said.

"He's telling us that the past although finished to us remains as a record of events on Earth to anyone interested enough to view it," Buick told him. "Constantly replaying itself. A continual process spawned by our reality. Am I right Father?"

He nodded. "The point I was attempting to make in my humble way is that with every passing day is created a record of yesterday. That is also true in the other Realms. Now bearing that in mind science tells us that the Earth is four and a half billion years old. It also suggests that life appeared on Earth approximately three and a half billion years ago. If you try to imagine that Earth history continues to repeat itself over and over since the very beginning four and a half billion years ago you begin to appreciate how much data the universe stores. Some claim that is the reason our universe is expanding. In order to accommodate and store this vast amount of knowledge."

"And this data storage is relevant because?" Maddox had been quiet watching and listening to the others. It wasn't that she was disinterested in what O'Malley was telling them more that she felt like an audience of one as if listening to a radio debate.

"I wish I knew," he said quickly. "Perhaps it's relevance is for God. Certainly someone who watches over humanity."

Desmond Hope was also unhappy. Maybe because hearing so much that went beyond anything he had ever encountered challenged his training as a psychiatrist. Or perhaps it was because as a psychiatrist the possibility that patients were less likely to have been suffering delusions than he might have believed making his diagnosis of their conditions wrong. Not that he hadn't treated them all with more open-minded thinking than his colleagues might have done. His personal encounters with the supernatural made him more open, but what O'Malley was telling them was a can of worms. How any of the people in the room would not be changed forever after learning about Dimensions, Realms, and a constant record of history able to be viewed by anyone with such a capability. What that might mean for patients impossible to grasp.

"You look concerned Desmond," O'Malley said.

He shook his head, "I was thinking about my patients and what some tell me. What they claim they either saw, heard, or experienced. They could be telling me accurate information and I might be disbelieving them because that's what I and my sister are trained to do. Our diagnosis was askew because we did not share what you have told us today. I'm hoping that we haven't done irreparable damage to anyone."

"But you're aware of supernatural entities," Hughes added. "You must give people plenty of rope before deciding whether or not they're insane."

Hope's creased expression was like someone stepped on his toe. "You're what people call a dinosaur aren't you detective?"

"Very possibly." Hughes replied without offence.

"Yes and no. It is true that our appreciation of the supernatural element affecting our world is always taken into consideration when we diagnose patients. Much more so than any ordinary psychiatrist, but what we have heard today is a massive game changer. The entire process of analysis needs to be comprehensively revamped. There is now so much for us to consider I'm not sure where to begin."

His sister leaned against him placing a hand on his shoulder, “We know that we have helped them. None have suffered as a consequence of visiting us.”

“I agree,” O’Malley said. “Your treatment is more likely to have helped them than their discovering that a bogey man really does exist. Not everyone has the capacity to accept what I am telling you. Hence the Church has seen fit to keep it from the public.”

“Would you notice if a patient were like us?” Dukes asked.

“Perhaps, after they were attending our clinic for a long time, but we’ve never identified anyone that we suspected of being touched by a supernatural entity.” It was clear from his expression that what he had learned had moved him, not just in regards patients but also at a more personal level. How he viewed life in general could no longer be fixed to the reality surrounding them. There was so much more and wished he could see it all for himself. At least he had a sister with whom to discuss what they had just learned.

"I know this is a lot to take in, but it needed to be done." O'Malley told them.

Hope shook his head, "I'm sure we all understand that Father. However, what you have just described makes our lives feel almost delusional. We're all happily carrying on our routines when in reality they're totally pointless. Everyone should be aware of the supernatural threat. Everyone."

"You are quite wrong our lives are important and significant to the natural balance. Without us much would change for the worse. Human lives are as significant to the natural order as any other element in the cosmos. The Church has kept the lid on the supernatural for a reason that has stood the test of time. To suddenly reveal the truth even now would cause world-wide panic that the authorities will be unable to control. That would do nothing to help the situation other than to add more adversity."

"I'm not sure the Church is not under-estimating the public's ability to adapt."

O'Malley understood. Heck he had even argued the same centuries ago and only gradually come round to the attitude shared by the Church. "You think the general public will not react the way you are reacting?"

Hope stared back as if he'd been kicked in the shin. "I thought we took your revelations very well."

"Really?" He replied. "You and this small group alone in London are aware of supernatural entities. You've just learned about other Realms. You now also appreciate that our spirits are immortal. That they journey to other Realms after we die and that they may return here. Something I remain unaware what that is dependent upon. Wish I did. However, this small group is also able to help one another as a group which is very important. A majority of the general public do not have people they can rely upon or who they would trust with their lives. The assessment of the general public's reaction to what I just told you remains firm as far as the Church is concerned. Please avoid spreading news about anything you have learned from me. It is vital we keep this secret to protect our world."

"I think you're correct Father," Hughes said staring at the others. "We all know how people react to even the slightest change to their routine and this is well beyond that. Take the pandemic as an example. Without leadership making the wearing of face masks mandatory we might have witnessed even more deaths. The delay before basic safety became a priority caused enough deaths. Then you've got the anti-vaxers who turned the whole thing with face masks into a political issue even while people were still dying. It was bonkers as far as I'm concerned. Now, can you imagine how people will react to the news that demons are real as are Illegras and different Dimensions and Realms! I don't know about you guys but me, I say not speaking to anyone outside this room about this makes sense."

"I also agree," Buick said casting in her vote recognising a need to take a mutually agreeable stance over issues that went way beyond the ordinary. Hughes had surprised her by not wanting to go public and she decided proved she could still be wrong. "No one must ever learn about the supernatural from any of us. I think we can agree that the Church has been at this a lot longer than us and has the experience to support its choices." Turning her attention to the Hopes she asked, "Are you in agreement with that?"

The brother and sister nodded their agreement. Expressions neutral making it difficult to know if they meant it. Buick had no choice other than to trust them. Besides O'Malley would have objected before now if he considered them a risk.

"Now that you've opened our eyes," Maddox said. "Is there anything else the Church can offer to fight these things?"

"Everything you need is in place."

"Everything?" She repeated uncertain what he meant by it. Agreed, they were now six instead of four a fifty percent increase in numbers. Then there were the priests sitting ready to come to their support at the first sign the Illegras began their attack. But the Illegras would number a hundred at the very least and those odds still appeared hard to swallow from where she was sitting.

"You are concerned that you will be unable to prevent the hive of Illegras swarming over your defences because you face superior numbers." O'Malley said as if reading her thoughts. “What you must add to any calculation is that humans are not alone on this world. The creatures you share it with are also a part of the army of your reality that will resist intruders. From the smallest to the largest they will help humanity push back against Earth’s enemies.”

“Hold on,” Dukes said. “Sorry, Father but you need to pass that by me again. Are you saying that animals, say cats and dogs will fight these things too?”

“Why are you so surprised aren’t they of this world. Is this not their home too? Aren’t animals and insects even more territorial than humans?”

Dukes turned to Buick with an expression that bordered between bewilderment and incredulity. Now even the animals and insects of the world would step up to fight the invaders from another Dimension. She shook her head as if at last reaching a point when she could accept nothing more.

"Actually, that makes more sense than the Realms," Buick said. "Humanity arrogantly calls itself the dominant species without actually knowing the capabilities or even being able to communicate with other species that share this world. It certainly does not surprise me to discover that they too will fight to defend their territory. However, I've never witnessed animals or insects attack any demon or Illegra that we've confronted to date."

"But many people have seen cats staring into apparent nothingness with their ears pricked up and their bodies ready to pounce. Why else do you think they behave in such a strange way if they are not seeing a supernatural entity?"

"Then I guess the next question has to be are there animals or insects that have been touched by supernatural entities?" Maddox asked.

O'Malley was beginning to enjoy himself. Broadening the minds of the group a satisfying experience. "Very, very few," he said. "Demons especially will do their utmost to kill any creature other than humans they make physical contact with partly because they do not want highly motivated and skilled predators with additional abilities here to greet them but also, animals are able to transfer their newfound abilities to their offspring."

"We should get a dog," Hughes said. "A big one."

"Does the Church have a plan?" Buick asked.

Moving to the partition that separated her office he leaned back against it. "I do." Taking a deep breath he allowed it to slip out quietly before beginning. "We need to capture one of the Illegra leaders. One that can be killed by the coloured blades I gave you."

"But you said that we couldn't do that?" Dukes said.

"That was before I figured a way it could be done." He said. The confusion and doubt on the faces of his audience prompted him to continue ignoring further questions. "We have an ideal prison here in this basement and the tools to do what is needed. I see this as an opportunity."

"How?" Hughes asked. "These things can walk through walls!"

"You have the prayer that I gave you earlier. It will prevent any Illegra from causing you physical harm."

"Why does it only work for only twenty-four hours?" Dukes asked.

"Twenty-four hours or a single contact."

"A single contact?" Buick asked.

"Every Illegra will recognise you are shielded, and that physical contact will destroy them. For that reason they will avoid making physical contact with you. Sadly, the shield will only offer you protection to destroy one Illegra that decides to ignore its own destruction. You can recharge the energy shield every twenty-four hours to have its protection again."

"And destroy another if we're attacked after twenty-four hours?" Dukes asked.

"Yes," he said. "I plan to write a solemn pledge handed down by God in a basement room chosen to capture the Illegra. Placing them on the ceiling, floor, and walls of the room will contain the creature and prevent its escape. In my briefcase shrouded in a blessed cloth is a mirror, it will act as the portal from which we will lure the creature here."

"So far, I can see us all locked in a room with one of humanity's most dangerous threats," Dukes said. "What I don't yet see is how we stop it going back through the mirror once it's here or how you're going to get information from it if that is what you intend to do?"

"One of you will place a crucifix on the mirror after it has arrived. Doing so will prevent its escape and block others from following. That part will be dangerous."

"But you said that the prayer you handed us will deter the Illegra physically touching us?" Hughes said.

"And so it will, but if you remember Illegras possess telekinetic abilities that allow them to move objects at their will. This is how it will attempt to escape. We must ensure the room it is captured has nothing it can use against us other than the mirror which the crucifix will stop from happening. Apart from that whoever is with me will need to be naked."

"What!" Dukes exclaimed.

"Otherwise it can use your clothes to throw you around the room. All without making physical contact," he said to them. "Please, you need to overcome your embarrassment. Only one of you needs to remove their clothes.

Buick saw the horrified expressions on the faces of the others and felt an urge to step-up. "This will prove dangerous so I think that I should be the one to do this with you Father."

"No way," Hughes erupted before catching himself and quickly apologising. "Sorry, Boss but you're needed here more than most. It should be me who goes with Father O'Malley."

"Not at all," Desmond Hope said. "You are a part of a team which operates effectively with all of you present. Mariam and I are individuals who have often operated alone against such monsters. I should be the one to join the Father."

"I agree," O'Malley said staring back at Desmond Hope.

"Whew," Dukes added. "That was close."

"You haven't yet explained what you intend to do with it?" Buick said. "I think we would all like to hear what happens after it's captured."

"I want to interrogate it to discover where the other portal to their dimension is hidden but more importantly where all the other Illegras are hiding, especially the oldest ones. They are the most formidable of our enemies."

"How can you obtain that kind of information from a supernatural entity whose sole purpose here is to destroy us all?"

"I have travelled far to find the necessary knowledge and believe I now have it." He replied, adding, "It lay in the Subterranean plane where it was placed more than fifteen hundred years ago. With it I can force the creature to tell us everything we need to defeat them."

There could be little doubt that O'Malley's claim boosted the spirits of all present. The idea that he could extract information from a deadly enemy that would ultimately lead to the destruction of all its contemporaries in their reality better than might have been expected.

"Sounds good to me," Dukes said turning to the others.

"We have a plan," Buick said.

CHAPTER SEVEN

Everyone appreciated that capturing an Illegra would not prove easy no matter how possible O'Malley made it sound. The sleeping accommodation adjoining the outer office had been selected to use for its capture. All furniture was removed while O'Malley drew strange words and symbols across the ceiling, walls, and floor. Placing a mirror still shrouded beneath a dark blessed cloth in the centre of the room.

Buick was in her office deliberating in her head the plan O'Malley had outlined for them. It was simple enough with a focus on the single Illegra he would draw into the adjacent room. However, what it did not include was the possibility of the appearance of more Illegras materialising before the crucifix was placed over the mirror or elsewhere in the building. He was unaware if

Illegras possessed an instinctive ability to find one another something she figured highly likely. Additionally, the fact it would be an ancient leader possibly meant it had a personal guard. Blocking off its personal guard would alert them that their leader was somehow threatened. She could imagine a small army of Illegras arriving through mirrors and reflective material on the floor above to rescue their leader. Anyone who stood in their way would be killed either by their soul being sucked out of them or physically torn apart. Not a pretty picture by any stretch of the imagination. How such an incident could be kept secret difficult to gauge depending on the number of people using the floor.

It was odd how coincidence sometimes operates the phone on her desk suddenly rang interrupting her thoughts. It was the head of maintenance Jonny Doyle. An infestation of rats on the floor above, the sub-basement had forced him to have it cleared of personnel until the pest control people arrived. Doyle asked if they were also visible at her lower basement level she said not. He figured someone must have brought something in that attracted them as the entire floor was covered by them. He had never seen so many. His advice was that she remain in their offices until he phoned to say they had been cleared. After placing the phone back on its cradle she was reminded of something O'Malley had pointed out. Every creature on Earth was an enemy of the Illegra, but whether that meant the rats had arrived because of their plan to capture a supernatural entity appeared so wild it went beyond imagination. Yet for what other reason had the rats come.

Stepping to her doorway to warn the others about the rats she took in how the others appeared. Maddox alone quieter than usual as she tapped at her computer keyboard. Still feeling the effects of her encounter with an Illegra who arrived from images in a dream. Compartmentalising the experience would take time, but at least she had participated during O'Malley's short education. What they had all learned altered the way they viewed their reality to a point that no longer resembled anything before they had listened to him.

Hughes was also alone tapping at his keyboard. Buick often felt he more than most had to struggle hardest to accept what they were all learning. Yet his acceptance of O'Malley's explanation appeared to have gone more smoothly than she expected. His challenges and desire to learn more growing obvious. Possibly given that they had all memorised an initially unrecognisable prayer and the paper on which it was written disappeared in a puff of smoke had sparked something deep within him. The final proof he needed to accept everything O'Malley told them. Dukes and Mariam Hope were together talking in low tones as if avoiding disturbing the peace. She couldn't hear what they were discussing but from their body language she guessed it was nothing serious. Calling for their attention she warned them not to leave the office to go to the sub-basement because of rats.

"Is that anything to do with what Father O'Malley mentioned?" Dukes asked.

Buick shrugged, "Could be. We need to remain vigilant just in case Illegras are able to communicate with each other even through protected walls. My guess is that this creature the Father intends to capture has bodyguards and once it goes missing they're going to search for him."

She left the outer office stepping into the corridor and headed for the adjacent room to warn O'Malley and Hope about the rats. O'Malley did not appear surprised.

"When will you be ready?" She asked.

"We're ready now. Desmond only needs to remove his clothing."

"What about you Father?" Hope asked.

"The clothes I wear have been blessed over many centuries and are impervious to anything from other dimensions."

Odd how something amusing can suddenly move through all an individual's mental filters at a serious time and make them smile. That's what happened with Buick as she imagined O'Malley's clothes never being washed over the past fifteen hundred years. He saw her smile and his eyes showed a question.

"Sorry Father," she said. "I just recalled something personal." Moving quickly on she looked at Hope, "I've left a chair outside this room for you to place your clothes. No one will enter while they're on it to save you any embarrassment."

"Thank you," he said.

"Is there anything else you need Father?"

"I want you to all repeat the prayer you have memorised in ten minutes time. You only need do it the once for its protection. Should any Illegras appear the Lord's prayer should suffice to shield yourselves."

"Should we gather outside this room?"

He shook his head, "No need this will be an impregnable cocoon to them. No getting in or out. I suggest you remain in your offices. Keep together to be as powerful as you can be." O'Malley sounded as if he was anticipating some kind of rescue squad appearing.

"How long will this take?"

"No more than an hour," he said.

"Pest control is on its way," she said.

"That has already been dealt with." She turned to leave when he said, "Superintendent."

She stopped with the door open, "Thank you and your people for all you have done and are doing."

With a nod she stepped out the room and closed the door. Returning to her own office she used the seat behind her desk and pondered on O'Malley's thanks. Sometimes overthinking things has the potential for people to read into remarks or actions more than was intended. Yet it sounded as if O'Malley had been determined to thank her because something bad was about to happen to either of them. Being immortal meant chances were she was the one on the receiving end of any bad. With a shake of her head she cast the negativity aside to favour that he was simply exhibiting gratitude. Oddly it wasn't sufficient to completely eliminate a sense of approaching dread.

O'Malley placed Hope's clothes on the chair outside their room and closed the door after his return. The central heating kept the room warm enough for the doctor not to feel cold but that didn't stop him from having goosebumps over what was about to happen. Gripped in the palm of one hand a crucifix given him by O'Malley that he had to place on the mirror immediately after the first Illegra made its appearance. Sneaking in behind the creature while O'Malley distracted it should have been simple enough, but his nakedness made it strangely more awkward. Humans were no longer accustomed to acting when naked other than in the bedroom he thought. He had once read somewhere that humans began wearing clothes around 170,000 years ago after the second ice age. The scientists coming to that conclusion by identifying when head lice turned to body lice due to clothing. Not that any of it was relevant to his current situation. Why he had bothered to learn so much useless information suddenly over such a long period of time challenged his own sanity.

"Are you ready Desmond?" Father O'Malley asked. "Have you repeated the prayer I gave you?"

No he had not. He'd been thinking about head lice instead. Quickly correcting his mistake he said the prayer. "I have now."

O'Malley nodded as he stood near the mirror in the centre of the room. An Illegra takes a minute to come through as a wisp of smoke and needs to materialise into a physical being before a second may follow. Hope had ten seconds in which to place the crucifix on the mirror before the smoke changed to a physical form. Chanting another set of unfamiliar words Hope listened as the priest repeated himself over and over. Initially nothing happened but O'Malley did not stop or pause he continued with the chant doing so for a full twenty minutes until a wisp of smoke became visible spiralling up from the mirror as its glass blackened. The sound of rushing air suddenly filled the room like a scream. Yet Hope felt none of it the air around him as still as it had been moments ago. The smoke grew above the mirror like a genie freed from the lamp in Sinbad. The smoke a dark grey green in colour. Hope suddenly wondered how to know when the last of the smoke was through? O'Malley hadn't told him. He could not place the crucifix on the mirror until then otherwise this attempt would prove a complete waste of time and alert the Illegra to what they were trying to do. The smoke kept coming rising into a large cloud high above the mirror as Hope began to sweat his nakedness not helping. Ripples of water began to run down his face and body before he realised the heat in the room had increased, that it wasn't his nerves. The frame around the mirror glowing as if it were an electric fire.

"Now!" O'Malley shouted.

Hope acted without thinking leaping the dozen feet between him and the mirror before placing the crucifix in place. Darting backwards as the creature began to materialise in its natural form. Thin stick like arms and legs first with ball sized elbow and knee joints protruding proudly before its fluid head and body shape like that of a jelly mould wobbled into view. Its head neck and torso all indistinguishable as their erratic movements merged and unmerged without any sign of regular pattern. Only its yellow eyes and toothless mouth revealed where its head was at any moment. Immediately it spotted O'Malley a deep grumble belched from its mouth. Turning away it spotted Hope. It's moving outline rearing up high over him as if about to attack. The long talons on its hands lifting high about to strike. Hope raised an arm to shield himself ready to die. Even as he did so he recited the Lord's prayer.

Eyes closed. Naked body tense. Frozen on the spot.

O'Malley's words reached through his dilemma and fear softly at first but steadily rising in power. The Illegra turned away back towards the priest glancing at the mirror and crucifix it bellowed noisily. Yet above the bellow O'Malley's words repeated themselves. Hope opened his eyes shocked to find himself alive and surprised to see the creature kneeling before the priest. For the first time the doctor realised that the creature was blue in colour. The same shade of blue as the blade in O'Malley's right hand that he was using as an orchestra conductor. The Illegra with its fluid outline appeared to succumb to the priest.

The first sign that O'Malley had an Illegra next door to their office reached Buick when the Illegra bellowed. Everyone in the room stopped what they were doing and stood stiffly upright. The atmosphere suddenly electric as they listened for the slightest indication that the priest needed help. Nothing.

"It's begun," she said. "Recite the prayer ready your blades."

They did as instructed while taking up the coloured blades. Not knowing what to expect only increased the fearful excitement they all shared. Strangely, none wondered if they would survive. None other than Buick that is. Yet if that was to be her fate then so be it she intended to make a good account of herself. The silence that followed the bellow felt ominous charged with an indefinable tease of imagination. Knowing something was about to happen while not knowing what it might be was a challenge too. The sound unfamiliar. They remained silent as their ears assessed what they were hearing. Analysing while attempting to match it to something familiar. Nothing. Multiple high-pitched squeals and deep barrelled bellows suddenly erupted right outside the door before something heavy thudded against it. Making it shudder and shake so violently it appeared ready to throw itself off its hinges. Everyone tensed ready to fight or die.

The door burst open and an Illegra came through the entrance with half a dozen rats clawing at its skin head to toe. Its fluid head neck and body indistinct above its skinny legs with their large protruding rounded knees. No one moved too startled to do so. Besides, the Illegra was obviously in pain as it fought the rats. Stabbing them with its talons and casting them aside until the floor around it was littered with bloodied corpses and intestines. When finished it turned to them its arms outstretched and talons dripping with blood. Bellowing briefly it moved towards them.

"No one move," Buick said. "It can't hurt us. It can't touch us."

Hughes was never one to ignore an opportunity which is

precisely what he figured their situation was before throwing himself at the creature. Knife raised as he aimed for its head. The Illegra side stepped its fluid outline distorting where its head was located confusing Hughes so much he hesitated stabbing the creature. The knife raised in his hand frozen like a statue. A moment later he brought it hard down on the creature's foot. The blade slicing through its skin so easily it penetrated the floorboards beneath and jammed itself there. A loud shriek burst from it before a second blade found its head and silenced it forever. Quickly turning to a wisp of smoke it disappeared.

Maddox looked at him. "Why should you have all the fun."

A second Illegra stumbled in fighting off more rats as they clawed and bit at its flesh. Before it got more than a few steps into the office Buick drove her blade into its head. Assessing that its bright yellow eyes and toothless mouth where her blade needed to strike. The creature didn't have time to collapse before it disappeared, and the rats scurried back outside.

Mariam Hope joined her, "Are you alright?"

"Apparently," she replied looking back at the others. "Let's take this outside, there's more space and our little friends seem to be doing pretty well."

Following closely behind her they were confronted by a stairwell swarming with rats and half a dozen Illegras. A battle between the two species taking place right in front of them. The rats were losing but kept coming. Kept climbing over their enemies to bite and gnaw at their unearthly bodies. Losing or not the rats were hurting the creatures and importantly distracting them. The shrieks and angry bellows given out by the Illegras confirmation.

For a moment Buick questioned whether to attack the nearest creature or to leave it for the rats. Quickly she decided to attack and raced towards it blade raised ready to strike. A thrust between its eyes as it turned and saw her caught it momentarily off guard. The blade sliced easily into its head and for a brief moment she thought it oozed a colourless liquid before disappearing in a puff of smoke. Hughes rushed by trying to avoid the rats occupying space on the stairs as he lunged at the next Illegra missing its head. The blade tearing into its torso while its head moved upwards on its wobbly uneven body. With a ferocious strike it cut the air with its long talons and struck Hughes chest. The explosion that erupted as a consequence destroyed the Illegra in an instant while Hughes staggered backwards down the steps unscathed. The rats dropped to the floor their victim suddenly gone and quickly found another.

“The Father warn us they exploded like that,” he said over his shoulder.

“Keep going,” Buick said close behind with the others following. Underfoot the rats were heading up the stairs moving faster than any human as they disappeared towards the next level.

The sight that confronted them surreal as they emerged onto the sub-basement corridor. A little wider than the basement wide enough for half a dozen to stand shoulder to shoulder. The stench of death hit them with a fearsome ferocity that took their breath away. Ahead at least thirty Illegras stood killing off the remains of the rat army. The dead bloodied bodies torn apart by lethal talons piled high around their fluid torsos while they continued to hack and stab at the remaining few who even now threw themselves at the creatures in a futile effort to delay them further. With more than two thousand of their dead demanding vengeance

Buick and her team watched as the last few fell among their own kind. When the slaughter was over the creatures turned and stared at the humans.

"This doesn't look promising," Hughes said as they formed a line across the sub-basement corridor. Blades ready as they recited the Lord's prayer.

"I'll lead," Hughes said.

"No," Buick said. "Your prayer protection won't work a second time. Stay behind us."

Never one to step back from a confrontation Hughes hesitated, but the women surrounded him a dangerous defiant obstacle as the Illegras stared unmoving in their direction. Buick momentarily wondered what they might be thinking. How they viewed the humanity and whether they were as scared of death as the people confronting them.

"What are they waiting for?" Dukes said.

The silence that followed painstakingly long in their minds while only thirty seconds in reality. The answer was as unexpected as it was gory and repugnant as a dead rat lifted from the floor as if by a giant invisible hand.

"Hit the deck!" Buick yelled throwing herself down the others following as corpses and entrails of rats suddenly filled the air. Hurled at them so hard contact would have smashed their skulls. Their speed of travel creating a brief vacuum that robbed them of air. The sound of the rats rushing overhead like a passing locomotive before they impaled into the stairwell wall. Quickly filling up the stairwell with shattered bodies until it became impassable. When it was over Buick gasping for air looked up at the Illegras moving steadily towards them. No one had the breath to recite the Lord's prayer and for a brief moment she felt ready to give up. To accept they were finished. That they had lost.

A new sound and sensation then plucked at her hearing as she watched the Illegras come to a halt just a dozen feet away and spin round. What happened next a blur of sounds. Voices, screams and deep barrelled bellows merged as one as the air filled her lungs once again and breathing returned. Around her the team too were regaining their strength Hughes already rising unsteadily onto his feet. Puffs of smoke denoting Illegra deaths began to appear behind the supernatural line up as Hughes helped Buick off the floor. They were under attack from behind but who? She marvelled with relief. Even as she did three Illegras closest to her turned their attention back towards IMP and charged. The first striking at her with its long deadly talons and dying in an explosion of bright light as the other two came up behind. The first catching her arm with a single blow that sliced open her bicep with a crimson belch that spurted and retched over Hughes.

As another Illegra slashed at her head Maddox blocked the attack with her blade and severed the talon clean off its hand. The creature jumped away trailing its injured hand.. Dukes and Mariam charged the Illegra that wounded Buick and between them slashed furiously right and left at it pushing it back towards the dwindling numbers of Illegras.

Hughes lay Buick on the floor and tore a sleeve off his jacket. Tying it round her bicep. The pulsing flow of blood needed immediate medical attention, but the stairwell behind was blocked by dead rats and the Illegras still fought in front of them. Beside them Maddox stood guard watching the others joining the fight with whoever had suddenly appeared from another stairwell.

Buick tried to focus to offer help, but blood loss made everything fuzzy around her. "What's happening?"

Hughes looked towards the depleted Illegra forces and smiled grimly, “The bad guys are getting their arses kicked Boss.”

“What about the others?”

A sudden roar from the battle made them both look towards the rush of men in dark blue boiler suits cut through the last of the Illegras. Their leader coming to a halt just in front of them a long golden blade in his hand. “Your friends are safe the enemy is defeated.”

Hughes read the logo on the man’s chest ‘Pest Control’.

“Thank God,” she said before passing out.

CHAPTER EIGHT

Acceptance

When Buick woke she discovered herself in a hospital bed. Marshal sat alongside wearing a warm smile as her eyelids fluttered open.

"Hi, there sleepy head," he said.

"What happened?"

"Your people won against whatever those things were," he said.

"Gosh I feel as if I was hit by a train," she said trying to push herself up before realising her left arm from the bicep down was missing. Wrapped in bandages the stub of her arm stared back at her as if waiting for acknowledgment. She could only stare at it in disbelief. Realisation would come as she mentally grappled with the injury as well as the reason for its loss.

"I'm so sorry Betty, there was nothing they could do to save your arm. You had gangrene when you reached the hospital. No one had ever seen it spread so quickly." His tone gentle soft attempting to soothe the horror.

Her head returned slowly to the pillow as tears welled in her eyes running silently down her cheeks. Marshal took her hand in his and squeezed it gently. "You're alive that's what counts."

She couldn't speak. Recalling O'Malley's thanks. He had known or suspected something bad would happen to her. She guessed there had been nothing he could have done to prevent it. It was the natural order that she lost her arm. Did that mean fate was real? If she had been on Alpha Centauri could she witness losing her arm again and again? Shaking her head Marshal misinterpreted the action believing he had said something wrong.

"I wish I'd been there to help you," he said.

"You're here when I need you most," she said.

He leaned forward and gently kissed her on the lips. "I hope you'll always want me close."

"But I've lost an arm, a hand. I'm disfigured," she said uncertainly.

"You're still beautiful to me," he said.

She didn't want to cry but the moment overwhelmed her, and she burst into a flood of tears that made him hold her as she shuddered and shook.

***

The next day O'Malley paid her a visit. He appeared tired certainly not immortal. The burden of what had happened to her clearly weighing heavily on him. "I'm sorry you lost your arm. You didn't deserve this."

"You knew didn't you?" She asked without malice. He could not have prevented it and telling her might have made her react differently. As it was they had achieved the right result.

Defeated overwhelming odds and secured the future of their reality. At least for now.

"I know you understand," he said. "We are both pawns in a much larger game of cosmic chess than either of us can imagine."

"Did you manage to find anything out from the Illegra you captured?"

He nodded face grim, "We destroyed the portal last night. None of the creatures remain including Dang's wife and the creature we captured."

"So why do you still look like we have a problem?"

"Perhaps because it was too easy. I expected more, but even the Russians are retreating from the Ukraine. So it is good news all round."

"And yet?"

"Something keeps nagging at me that I cannot yet grasp." He shook his head. "Never mind, how are you feeling?"

"I spent an entire night crying and feeling sorry for myself and now I'm all cried out and ready to live my life afresh. They're going to give me a prosthetic arm that will balance me out as far as the disfigurement is concerned."

"You won't need it," he said.

She initially thought he was being kind claiming her physical appearance didn't need balance, then realised there was something more. "What do you mean?"

"In some ways the Illegra that sliced off your arm did you a service. It handed you a weapon." He paused momentarily allowing his words to sink in. "Whenever you face any creature from the supernatural a powerful forearm and hand will materialise providing you with a physical means to defend yourself."

"Did I lose my arm for that reason?" She asked her mind quickly racing to the most logical explanation.

"Things always happen for a reason Superintendent. I suspect that the power who watches over us knows when we need more than what we possess to defeat our enemies. Wear a prosthetic limb but beware that it will be discarded and replaced the moment you are threatened by any supernatural entity."

"How do you know that?" She asked. "Can you at least tell me?"

Having the discretion to reveal more about their reality meant that he was not limited by oaths of secrecy. "You are already aware of the Astral and Sub-Terranean planes. There are also an infinite number of Realms in which the spirits of our ancestors, brothers, and sisters dwell. Journeying to them when asleep is how I am able to discover so much. It took me a very long time to appreciate why I should sleep even though it's physically unnecessary that I do so."

"And do these spirits tell you what will happen in the future?"

"Only rarely," he said. "It is however where I discover the means and methods by which we can defeat our supernatural enemies." A sudden wave of tiredness flowed over her making her blink to keep her eyes open. "I can see that you need to rest. Be assured I will always be here for you."

"Thank you Father," she said.

***

Marshal was alone in his office awaiting the consent of a search warrant before paying the Burns household a visit. The missing detectives were still missing and even though the threat from the supernatural had apparently been eliminated his investigation remained ongoing. A mug of hot coffee on his desk to help with a couple of headache pills steamed gently in front of him. The headaches had begun soon after the encounter with the Illegra rushing from where Maddox had been sleeping. It had knocked him into a wall before disappearing. The brush of its body against his face never forgotten. He had said nothing to anyone else choosing to ignore the contact. But the headaches had become more frequent and intense. He had considered discussing them with Buick but figured she had her own problems to deal with and telling her about headaches seemed a little pathetic. Besides the tablets gave relief for a time.

Returning his attention to the investigation he browsed the evidence on his computer screen. Statements from the Burns pair the only real lead they had. What didn't make sense was two burly detectives disappearing upon immediately leaving. Knowing that Emily Burns was a member of the Satanic Chapel which itself appeared inextricably involved with the supernatural suggested clues relating to their disappearance might be found at the Burns residence. One way or another he was going to find out what happened to the two men.

An hour later with the search warrant in hand Marshal and a team of detectives and uniformed officers visited the Burns address. It was late evening with the Moon high in a twinkling cloudless sky while a chill northly breeze kept the temperature around zero.

Arthur Burns opened the door and appeared surprised to see so many officers," How can I help you?"

"We have a warrant to search your premises Mister Burns," Marshal told him showing him the warrant before stepping inside without further discussion.

Emily Burns came out of the kitchen to see what was happening and looked aghast at the sight of so many police entering her home. Her red head beauty growing dark with outrage. "Arthur, what is this all about?"

"They have a warrant to search our home," he replied weakly.

"Why would they want to do that?"

Marshal stopped in front of her, "I think you know more about the missing detectives than you're willing to share. You can stop this search now by telling us what you know."

"That's ridiculous," she said. "We've told you everything!"

"Not everything," he said. "Our detectives cannot go missing from your front door to their car without you seeing or hearing something."

"You're insane," she said stepping away from him as if feeling threatened. For a moment it appeared that she might lose her customary cool, but somehow managed to hang onto it.

"I'm going to find them Mrs Burns even if I have to turn this house inside out doing so."

"Sir, you need to come and see this," one of his detectives called.

He followed the sound of the detective's voice to a back room full of paintings. They hung on all four walls while the room itself was empty of furniture apart from a small dais in its centre. Twelve by twelve inches in size enclosed in thin wooden frames more than two dozen decorated the walls. As Marshal studied them he realised they were almost identical. A black gated entrance to the side of a grey boulder mountain. Any differences related to the figures standing in front of the entrance.

The abrupt sound of high-pitched whispering hit Marshal hard making him reel back from the paintings. All at once multiple whispers filled his head. A single word repeated over and over. Help!

"Are you alright sir?" A detective asked.

"Fine," he said quickly regaining composure. Call it instinct but Marshal felt an overwhelming sense of presence as if surrounded by dozens of people vying to catch his attention. Resisting an urge to throw up as his headache returned now turning into a full-blown migraine he followed the paintings along the wall until he found what he had been searching for. The detectives standing outside the entrance. Removing himself quickly from the room he used his mobile to contact Maddox explained what he had found and asked her to attend.

"Arrest the Burns and take them down to the station," he told his detective.

Maddox and the other members of IMP arrived within the hour. Marshal still felt too weak to return to the house and told his detective to show them the paintings.

They stared at the oil paintings only half believing what Marshal had told them. That somehow the paintings were of real people held captive in the artwork. He didn't know how it was possible just that their call for help was real as far as he was concerned.

Maddox had already asked O'Malley to meet them at the address. He arrived shortly behind them spoke to Marshal before being ushered inside.

The priest studied each of the paintings in turn which took more than an hour. When finished he called Maddox to one side, "Most of the people in the paintings are dead."

She frowned, "But not all of them?"

"The detectives are the only living spirits but they're both weak. They cannot survive much longer."

"Do you know how to get them out?" She asked ignoring the fact they were discussing something so unbelievable so impossible that even her imagination found it difficult to cope.

"I can make it happen," he said. "But I must be alone. Get Marshal to clear the house. There cannot be any other human vibrations within twenty feet of this painting otherwise the distortion will prevent their materialisation."

"You want us outside as well?" She asked.

Of course," he replied staring at the painting with the detectives.

The house was cleared with a ring of police surrounding it waiting for what no one was sure. Marshal and Maddox stood together with the bulky Hughes and beautiful Dukes behind them.

"How long is this going to take?" Marshal asked as a chill wind slapped against his face reminding him it was still winter.

"It'll take as long as it takes," Maddox replied stiffly uncertain that even O'Malley knew the length of time it would take him to rescue the detectives.

Fifteen minutes later O'Malley appeared at the front of the house with two tall figures behind him. Their unsteady movements making the nearest officers rush forward to help.

“I’m starting to believe nothing I see is what it is,” Marshal said staring at the two detectives with unconcealed astonishment. After a moment he began walking towards Harringay and Davies as they stopped at the rear of an ambulance and were checked over by paramedics. His headache subsiding as quickly as it had begun.

***

Helen Frobisher sat at Buick’s bedside. Arm in a sling but looking better than Buick expected considering she was in recovery from a gunshot wound. Frobisher was eager to return to work after learning all that had happened since being shot. The tales of encountering an army of Illegras at the office without her and being rescued by priests from Rome dressed up as pest controllers made the impression of what she missed only more exciting. Frobisher wanted to know every little detail. Buick admired her enthusiasm and really could never recall being half as enthusiastic at the outset.

The entrance of Maddox and Hughes interrupted further discussion and came with some relief for Buick. Although she conveyed an acceptance of her new disability it remained a work in progress and each memory of the day her arm was taken only heightened the pain she felt.

Hearing the news that the missing detectives had been found provided some comfort. Another part of the puzzle resolved. Buick wondered if it were enough to satisfy O'Malley or if his instincts continued to haunt him that they were still missing something.

"All we now need is for you two to return to work to begin a new investigation," Maddox said.

"What about Arthur and Emily Burns?" Buick asked.

"Marshal has them in custody, "Hughes said. "Clearly there are issues that need to be ironed out. We don't want press headlines highlighting that people were kidnapped and spirited into oil paintings. Not sure how they're going to resolve that one, but luckily it's not our problem."

"Where's O'Malley?" Buick asked.

"Haven't seen him since he freed the detectives," Maddox said. "I'm sure he'll be in contact when he's needed again."

"Did he say anything about there being more to do?"

Maddox surprise was obvious, "No!" Her thoughts then quickly moving to Suffolk the MP suspected of involvement with the Russian oligarch. "Marshal informed SO Fifteen, the terrorist bunch about the MP. As far as I know they're dealing with that part, but unsurprisingly we haven't heard anything more."

Buick shrugged. "If O'Malley has anything else troubling him I'm sure we'll be the first to know.

While Buick and Maddox discussed O'Malley. Waiting patiently outside her room Dukes and Hughes used the empty seating available. The ward was quiet with just a single face masked nurse moving around from room to room. The detectives wore their face masks as recommended at the hospital entrance. The pandemic was not over but it had been tamed to a point that life had begun to return to normal.

While Hughes flipped through missed messages on his mobile Dukes slipped her own mobile into a pocket and stretched her longs legs in front of her. At about the same time she spotted four colourless individuals moving towards them along the corridor. Blinking once, twice she pushed herself up and stared hard in their direction. No visible sign of legs and a black and white appearance. Spirits she thought to herself.

"Billy, can you see them?" She asked as if praying he would.

Hughes looked up in the direction she was staring. An empty corridor with some equipment either side nothing more. “What do you see?”

“Black and whites,” she said.

“How many?”

“Four,” she said.

They entered the ward and appeared to notice her stare. Silently they approached coming to a halt directly in front of them.

“They’re right in front of us Billy.” She said. Seeing something no one else does is not normal and in any other circumstances would likely be considered a sign of insanity. With that mind she tried to calm herself as the entities stared directly back at her just a few feet away.

“Speak to them,” he said. “Ask them why they’re here.”

She did as he asked. An onlooker would have seen her talking to empty air something she was well aware. Thankfully there were none. The spirits stared blankly at her as if not hearing or perhaps unwilling to converse.

"What are they doing?" Hughes asked.

"Nothing. I'm not sure they can hear me. They're just staring back as if I'm insane. I'm beginning to think I might be!"

The nearest spirit then mouthed something slowly as if hoping she could lip read. It appeared to be male which even without features seemed a reasonable guess. However, with large dark eyes studying her she felt it possible to feel his gaze. Mouthing something else Dukes studied his mouth, but the outline of his lips were too thin to read.

"Speak slower," she told him and with a gesture to her ears. "I cannot hear you. I'm trying to lip read."

The spirit then made gestures with its hands.

"It's using sign language to communicate," she said suddenly recognising what he was doing.

"Do you know any?"

"Some," she said and answered the question the spirit asked explaining how she had the ability to see them. Without any expressions to reveal its excitement she had to gauge its reaction from body language and the way the others around it behaved. They were definitely excited bobbing up and down on their misty whatever.

"Are you getting through?" Hughes asked.

"I think so, they seem glad to have made contact."

The spirit told her its name had been Tom Horton when alive in her physical reality. He was killed in a motoring accident back in 1926 and had been stuck in the in-between since then. The others around him were all from the same decade so they tended to stick together.

Dukes repeated what she had been told to Hughes. The big detective sighed, "Gosh, he's more than a hundred years old. What's he doing at the hospital?"

She asked. The spirit of Tom Horton replied using gestures that Dukes found familiar to British Sign Language she had learned. "They come here to find new spirits like themselves. He says it's a trauma for new spirits to accept their new reality. That some never do. Those who resist often turn into poltergeists or something else threatening because they're overwhelmed by anger.

"Can they help us fight Illegras and demons?" He asked.

"No," the reply came quickly back. "All they do is watch. It's not that they can't, it's just that they choose not to do so."

"Can any supernatural entities attack them?" He asked.

"Not in their experience they have an advantage over most, but Tom says they have enough of their own problems with angry spirits living among them. It's why they try to reach and help new arrivals before the anger takes hold."

"Bloody hell, just when you think you've moved on from all the shit this world hands out you find yourself in the in-between having to deal with more," Hughes grumbled. "Tell him I feel for him."

"I think they heard you," she said. "We can't hear them, but they can hear us."

The spirit of Tom Horton told her they had to leave. That a new spirit was coming, and they had to be ready to greet it. She asked if they could meet again, and his spirit said they would. Then they turned and continued down another corridor.

"Are you feeling better about the black and white people now?" He asked.

"A little," she said. "I'm just hoping I don't end up there. I got the distinct impression they're all very sad."

CHAPTER NINE

The missing detectives had proven unhelpful to the investigation headed by Marshal due to memory loss. How they ended up in an oil painting not even a blurred memory. What they did while in the oil painting unrecoverable. It was as if their lives had been paused together with their memories. Walking away from the Burns house then reappearing again inside the room inside an oil painting the end and start of their memories.

Arthur Burns said very little during his interview. Yes and no answers nothing more. The detectives interviewing him noted his blank expression and failure to make eye contact with either of them. Staring into nothingness his chosen tactic. While Emily Burns was a totally different animal. She objected and complained about everything as if doing so would eventually get her what she wanted. Released. A lawyer from the

Rotherbloom lawyers office in Pall Mall, one of the Top 100 firms in the country arrived within minutes of the Burns incarceration.

Money talks. Marshal figured as their lawyer a tall sophisticated late thirties hot shot called Leslie Case appeared. He wore a daring glint in his eyes that suggested even eye contact came at a cost. The fact that two missing detectives had been found at the Burns home indicated they had possibly been kidnapped by the homeowners. Needless to say Case did not see things that way. Emily Burns claimed she had not seen them sneak back into their home after pretending to leave or return to hide in their back room. Why they had done such a thing a mystery to her and her husband. Because the back room was not regularly used they could have remained in it for a month without being noticed. Also, noticing food and milk going missing was something she had ignored until their discovery.

It took a lot to rile Marshal who was known for his cool calm demeanour. Yet something about Case appeared to discover the button that agitated his irritation. For that reason the Superintendent found it harder than normal to suppress an increasing urge to say what he was thinking.

"I believe you've heard a very reasonable explanation," Case said. "Clearly your detectives were acting on their own initiative and for reasons only known to themselves chose to hide away at the Burns house."

"That is not what our detectives are telling us," He said.

"And what exactly are they telling you Superintendent?"

"They have no memory what happened to the between when they left the Burns home and were discovered days later in their back room."

"Convenient memory loss for them both, but their memory loss doesn't implicate Mr and Mrs Burns in their disappearance. You only have to compare the size of your detectives with the Burns to know it would have been an incredible feat for them to have overcome your detectives. At least that would be the conclusion of any reasonable individual. Now I suggest that you either release my clients or charge them."

Emily Burns had quietened down since the arrival of Case and sat quietly watching the proceedings. A smug confident smile and unflinching sparkle in her eyes that told Marshal she knew he was about to set them free.

Later as the man and wife left the police station with their lawyer Marshal watched from a window. The rain filled darkness quickly enveloping them, so their figures disappeared. They had known he could not reveal the truth about the oil paintings. The other paintings on the wall included more missing from the local area.

None ever found. After what he had gleaned from Maddox the detectives were the only ones to survive the experience. It had been galling to watch Emily Burns smug expression grow as he set them free. Returning to his desk he viewed the screen on his desk display the list of accountants killed by Conti with Burns the last mentioned and still alive.

Searching for a connection between them had so far proved futile. The firms that employed them were in general under different ownership and appeared, at least on the surface, free of scandal. The only possibility of something untoward rested with Vova Stepanov a Russian Oligarch suspected of laundering stolen billions through London. Marshal sighed at the thought of London being referred to as London-Grad because some of their own politicians benefitted by allowing numerous oligarchs to clean their money through the great city. Tarnishing it forever by doing so. Since the unwarranted Russian invasion of Ukraine loopholes had possibly shrunk the flow, but he doubted it had been completely eliminated. Too many fat cats in the City would be working hard to ensure that didn't happen.

Burns had been used by Stepanov very occasionally over the past two years but more in an advisory role than directly to 'cook' the oligarch's books. Even so, how that might have had anything to do with the list of dead accountants remained a mystery.

Marshal switched his screen to view Arthur Burns interview. The blank expression and unfocused gaze of the accountant made the entire process appear as if they were talking to a zombie. Yes and no answers limited any useful evidence to be gleaned from him. Switching to the interview of Emily Burns mirrored two different extremes. Burns wife could not stop herself talking complaining and being outraged until the arrival of their lawyer. The moment he stepped into the interview room she fell silent. It was creepy how that happened. The jump to silence created an eerie hush up to the moment the lawyer spoke.

Returning to the image of the list he studied it for the umpteenth time before an idea struck him. Just maybe he was looking at it from the wrong perspective. Maybe the list of dead accountants wasn't the real issue. Checking their names he discovered each was married. Emailing each of the detectives leading their individual murder investigations he asked for details of their wives together with a photograph if possible. After that he headed home.

The following morning around nine he returned to his office. No emails from the eight detectives involved in the murder list had yet been received. It wasn't until noon when two arrived within minutes of one another. The details of both wives were skimpy to say the least while their descriptions sounded similar. Tall, dark haired, pointed features. Good looking. Aged around mid-thirties. Not much to go on but it was a start. By four that afternoon the other detectives had answered his email. The only consistency the description of the wives. He contacted IMP and spoke to Maddox briefing her on his new theory that perhaps the wives were the real motive behind the murders. The limitations of his own investigation because of the supernatural angle meant he needed IMP to do the legwork as well as confront the supernatural beings that might be encountered. He promised to email her with the details provided by the other detectives.

***

Commander Brandown visited the IMP office to officially make Maddox temporary head of the team in Buick's absence. He gave a short speech in which he acknowledged Hughes and Maddox were of equal rank, but because IMP was a Metropolitan Police unit rather than belonging to British Transport Police he felt it more appropriate that a Met. Officer be handed the lead role. After he left them Maddox took up temporary occupation of Buick's office. Not because she wanted to flaunt her newfound status in front of anyone, but more because she longed for the solitude it offered.

She remained working quietly for the most part. Her head still dealing with turbulent emotions over the Illegra dream experience that made sleep something to be avoided. Even if it were an essential ingredient of the human cycle that allowed her to properly function. Yet lying in bed at night she found herself resisting the temptation to close her eyes something that had become a regular chore. Even knowing that the prayer she spoke each night would shield her from the possibility of an Illegra materializing within a dream it wasn't enough to placate her fears. At work her mood swings because she was not sleeping properly were obvious yet neither Dukes nor Hughes chose to discuss or offer sympathy. It was not wanted. For that reason Hughes contacted the Hopes and Mariam Hope offered to come across to visit Maddox without letting slip that he had been responsible for contacting her.

She arrived shortly after Maddox had spoken with Marshal and tapped at the door to Buick's office to say hello. Being separated by a glass partition from the others a necessary way for her to keep everyone at arm's length Mariam noted. However, she invited her in and offered some coffee which was duly accepted.

"I was passing by and wondered if you had heard anything about Arthur Burns. Desmond is curious after he and his wife were released?"

"I might have something," Maddox said. "Marshal cannot take his investigation too far towards the supernatural for obvious reasons, but has a new idea about the list of dead accountants and its relevance." She said placing a steaming mug of coffee in front of Mariam. "He began looking at the wives of the eight dead accountants and from their descriptions it's possible we are talking about eight Illegras. Their descriptions are very similar but because they're spread across the country the detectives in each case have not encountered more than one."

Mariam fidgeted on the seat, "But how is that possible. We destroyed the last portal and all the Illegras including the golden one returned to their Dimension?"

Maddox turned her screen around so that Mariam could read the descriptions of the wives detailed by officers from each of the murder investigations. When she finished reading, "It doesn't seem possible but details from eight different detectives relate the identical appearance to Dang's wife."

"And we know she is no longer with us because she returned when the portal was destroyed. Also Marshal visited and was told she had taken a holiday," Maddox said. "So, it appears that we're discovering an access that may be older than the portals we destroyed. What is interesting is that if there is another portal it means Illegras are only returned after the portal which brought them here is gone. They are totally reliant on it to maintain their presence in our reality and do not receive energy via other portals."

"I wonder if O'Malley realises that?" Mariam said softly almost to herself. "Do you think that means they can still install themselves in our dreams?" She introduced the question about sleep as if it were an aside without other motive.

Maddox shook her head, "Apparently the prayer we memorised will shield us from them. I've been using it myself and haven't encountered any."

"That's good to know, I'd hate to think they could reach us through dreams again."

Maddox fell silent. Her expression one of concentration as if weighing up the other woman through fresh eyes. She had also been a detective too long not to pick-up indications of ulterior motive.

"Are you coping?" Mariam continued.

"Fine," she said.

"Not sure how I'd cope if it happened to me," Mariam said.

"Did someone call you?" Maddox asked leaning back in the chair. Mariam's unexpected arrival suddenly feeling contrived. That and how their conversation had swung so easily round to sleep piqued her instincts.

"They're concerned," she said honestly. There was no point being anything else if she wanted to continue having the other woman's trust. "I want to help, and you look a little on edge."

"I'm coping," she said. "It's not easy but I'm sure I'll get over it eventually."

"Okay, but if you ever need a friend to talk with you have my number. Call anytime night or day."

Maddox studied her a moment, "Do you really think you can get the image of that thing out of my head?"

"What I think is that I can help you compartmentalise it. Mental scars are what they are. Impossible to completely remove but if you really want to move on with your life you need to let others in to help you do so. Over the past twenty years that much is something that I've learned. I don't guess that I can help you I know I can because I have done so with many others and because you and I share something few others have."

"Bet you've never had to deal with someone with being attacked by a nightmare," she said.

"True," Mariam admitted. "But horror comes in all shapes and sizes. What happened to you is only another horror story to me. Others have experienced what I consider worse and some much easier. How each of us successfully deals with a horror is what makes it a survivable experience. Because our awareness of it gives us an edge that we did not possess before it happened. You are now aware that Illegras can attack you through your dreams. Little wonder you probably try to avoid sleeping. However, and this is particularly significant. Your subconscious is also aware and will be prepared to defend you against such an attack."

"You're sounding like O'Malley. He talks about our subconscious as if it is a second individual living within us." Maddox said.

"It's not that our subconscious is a second individual, more that it's who we are when asleep. People have a duality about them as humans that in the spirit world re-engage into a single entity. Same person different reality. I often wonder if we could just get the two to re-engage here then just maybe our knowledge of both realities will prove to be a potent weapon. Trouble is that would go against Nature which wants us to remain in this reality split in two."

"Life has become so complicated since I joined IMP," she admitted.

"Discovering that what we see and hear is not all that's happening takes time to come to terms with. I know because it did for us. Though if I'm honest I'm not sure that any of us including our two brothers in France have fully come to accept everything we now know to be true."

"And that's after more than twenty years of knowing," Maddox said before sarcastically adding, "Thanks that really makes me feel better."

Mariam smiled and the detective grinned back. "You've just

joined the club. You're still just a newbie."

"Yeah, I guess it's my own fault for not joining IMP sooner."

"Do you want to sleep at our place tonight?" Mariam asked. "We have a spare room, and you will be safe with us."

She was about to decline then hesitated considering the alternative. Another broken night of sleep while alone in bed. The normal house sounds waking her playing with taught nerves. The prospect hardly riveting she accepted her offer.

Mariam rose from the seat, "I'll pick you up if you want?"

"No, I'll drive. I have your address. Thanks for this."

After Mariam had gone she told the others about Marshal's theory and provided the details of the dead accountants wives. "So, it appears possible that we're still faced by an Illegra threat."

"Do you want us to pay each of these wives a visit?" Hughes asked.

She shook her head, "Not at this stage. They're spread across the entire country. I've a better idea." She said, "Let's have a word with Mister Dang."

"But he's part of the Satanic Chapel. Not the sort to tell us anything useful," Dukes was quick to point out.

"Something Marshal told me about Arthur Burns intrigues me. He claimed that Burns behaved as if he were a zombie. Providing yes and no answers in a robotic manner. I'm wondering if his wife, a high priestess of some sort in the Chapel is controlling his mind. After the oil paintings incident with those detectives I'm beginning to believe anything's possible."

"If that's true why are we wasting our time going to check out Dang?"

"Because Dang's wife is gone we know as much from Marshal. Who released Dang this morning. Burns wife on the other hand is very much alive and well. If Dang was under mind control he might be free to talk to us now. If not then I want you two to make him think we're on his case and closing in. I don't care how you go about doing that and will take any heat if needed." She said.

"Sounds good to me," Hughes said with a nod of agreement from Dukes.

***

Philip Dang could not conceal his surprise at Hughes and Dukes appearance at his front door and appeared more than a little uncertain before inviting them in. The house was silent and in darkness except for a small glowing bulb in the kitchen.

"You're clearly saving on your energy bill," Dukes said.

"Is your wife home?" Hughes asked already knowing the answer.

"Why do you ask?" Dang replied.

"We'd like to ask her some questions too," Dukes said.

"She's out, but why you think she might be able to help you is beyond me. I take it you're here about the detectives recently found at the Burns house?"

"Partly," Hughes said. "We want to know about you're position in the Satanic Chapel?"

"What has that to do with your detectives?"

"You clearly misunderstand how this works," Dukes told him. "We're the police and we ask the questions you're the suspect and you answer them."

"Suspect!" He exclaimed taken aback. "Do I need a lawyer?"

"Only if you have something to hide," Hughes said. "Otherwise just answer our questions then we'll be out of your hair. Now what's your status in the Chapel?"

"I'm not very high, just one of many apostles."

"What does that actually mean?" Hughes persisted.

"I'm a believer that Satan was poorly treated by God and should be admired and respected for what he has given to the Earth and its people."

"Okay, this I must hear," Dukes said. "What did Satan bring to the table that attracts humanities admiration and respect?"

"He provided humans with critical thinking which challenged God. Our God wanted to deprive us of knowledge and by doing so, commit us to a life of mental slavery for the rest of eternity. Satan did us a big favour turning the tables on him with a single conversation."

"And is that it?" Dukes asked.

"Satan is recorded in the Bible as being responsible for the deaths of only ten people by comparison to God who killed more than two point three million. All because Satan understands human nature better than God and, for that reason, doesn't judge us for our human failings. With Satan we are all accepted unconditionally as his children. Any moral comparison between God and Satan leaves a clear message that Satan is the better of the two. Satan is the way to peace and contentment."

"And you believe this crap?" Dukes asked unable to stop herself smiling.

"Why shouldn't I the proof is evident each morning we awake. God dupes us while Satan attempts to save us from his beguiling moral temptations which he himself ignores."

Dukes had read that atheists followed a similar theory. Her Catholic upbringing resented what Dang had said which did not help with her judgment of him.

Before Hughes could ask another question the front door was heard to open and close as someone walked heavily along the hall towards the kitchen. Dang's wife suddenly appeared at the doorway. A brown leather handbag hanging from her right hand as she studied the two detectives.

"What's this?" She asked.

"The police want to ask you questions about the detectives that were recently found at Arthur's place," Dang said so quickly the words were almost unintelligible.

"Me!" She exclaimed.

Hughes figured it was one of those evenings when everyone received a surprise. Like he had just done when Martine Dang suddenly appeared at the kitchen door. The fact that his skin crawled while his spine tingled as a wave of hatred touched his senses reminded him what she really was. Fighting the urge to attack her he settled for asking a question, "Where have you been Mrs Dang?"

"I was visiting a friend," she said quickly adding. "Is that against the law?"

"Not yet," he replied. "As long as you left them alive."

Her eyes suddenly sparked with darkness that even the poor lighting could not conceal. Flicking a switch on the wall the ceiling lights suddenly lit up the room. "Have I answered all of your questions, if so I hope you'll leave us alone?"

Dukes was about to jump in with both boots when Hughes gently brushed her arm. "I think we'll have more questions for the both of you by tomorrow. Our investigation is moving quickly now that we've destroyed a couple of entrances. We have only one more to find then we'll definitely be back Mister Dang."

"I'm sure neither of us knows what you're talking about," he replied too weakly for his wife who glared at him.

"I'll show you to the door," she said turning on her heel and leading them out.

After they returned to the car Dukes in the driver seat asked, "Do you want to leave?"

He passed her a knowing look, "Not right away. Let's see if they decide to pay someone else a visit. Send Bran a text let her know what we're doing."

"Do you think that really was his wife?" Dukes asked.

"She's an Illegra. That much I know for sure, but whether she's the same as the one married to him I really can't say." He said without looking at her. "The hate was the same I experienced from the other one. It's overwhelming, so powerful it feels like it's weighing you down."

"Does it hurt?" She asked.

"Not hurt, it plays around with your emotions so that you're almost disorientated from reality. It's weird. In some ways I think they and I connect somehow, on another level. I can't explain it."

"I know the feeling," she sympathetically replied. "This world just gets crazier by the day. I'm not sure I could deal with what Bran had to contend with. The idea of falling asleep and being woken by one of those things on top of me gives me the shudders."

"You and me both." He said.

It didn't take long for the Dang's to appear. Striding quickly from the front door of their home to a dark Ford SUV parked outside. The rain began to fall again so Dukes used the wipers to see the direction they took.

"They're headed in the direction of the Chapel," Dukes said slipping into gear and moving away from the kerb with the sidelights glowing dimly. Not using headlights to help avoid being spotted. As the rain fell harder she was forced to use headlights and grumbled to herself for having to do so. The Dangs drove passed the Chapel headed East with the police keeping a discrete distance. Not too difficult given the poor weather conditions.

As they reached Chadwell Heath a suburb on the outskirts of London the Dangs vehicle slowed and indicated it was turning left. Dukes continued straight along the main road with Hughes craning his head round to ensure the Dangs didn't slip away behind them. Completing a U turn on an otherwise empty main road had them facing the right way as they slowly moved alongside the kerb opposite the road the Dangs had taken.

"It's a dead end," Hughes said straining his eyes through the heavy rain that thrummed incessantly against the roof of the car. "I can make out railings at the far end maybe a cemetery?"

"Can you see their car?"

"Yeah, it parked up next to the last house on the left," he said. Vehicles were parked either side in a cul-de-sac of terraced properties.

Lights shone from all but the last on the left. "Let's leave the car here and take a walk."

"I knew you were going to say that" she said. "Good job I'm wearing my waterproof hoodie otherwise I'd be complaining. Also, it's a good job I don't wear much make-up otherwise it would be running down my face making me look like an Illegra!"

"And this is you not complaining," he replied climbing out.

They strode across the main road without seeing any traffic. The rain continued in a ceaseless barrage that quickly matted Hughes hair to his scalp. Following the left side terraced housing as close to the front hedges as possible they approached the end house. Dukes stopped so abruptly it took Hughes by surprise.

"What's wrong?" He asked.

"It's the black and white spirit from the hospital. Tom Horton. He's in front of me."

"What does he want?"

Dukes watched as the spirit frantically gestured using sign language. "He's telling us to go back. It's too dangerous here."

It wasn't like the big detective didn't know that. His skin crawled and itched like a mad thing while his spine tingled so much he thought he'd been electrocuted. "Tell him we know, but we have a job to do."

"He's shaking his head," she replied. "He keeps saying it's too dangerous. I think we should listen to him."

Hughes reluctantly nodded in agreement, "Okay, but what are we going to tell Bran?"

The rumble of thunder emanating from dense grey clouds high above was followed by a flash of lightning. The occurrence immediately removed the black, white spirit that had appeared before Dukes. "He's gone."

"Guess he doesn't stay around when people heed his advice." Hughes said before interrupted by a terrified scream emanating from the end house.

The detectives looked at one another Dukes already aware that they had been given no choice. Hughes led, lifting the blade from a pocket as he pushed through the front gate. Another roll of thunder rocked the sky as more lightning flashed above the roof of the end house making its appearance all the more ominous.

“Before we go any further Billy I want you to know that I’m crapping myself.”

“Thanks, good to know I’m not alone.”

***

Bran Maddox was worried. Dukes and Hughes were headed into the unknown without support and something about the scenario didn’t feel right. A call to the Hopes quickly found her the resources needed to support them. Providing details of the location in Chadwell Heath the brother and sister headed out to join the detectives. As a precaution she also contacted Father O'Malley and warned him what was happening. He had listened patiently before telling her that he too would visit the suburb. Maddox sat back feeling a little better whilst wishing she did not need to remain at the office in the event things went pear shaped and a call to regular officers was needed.

The thought how she might react if she came face to face with another Illegra continued to unsettle her. Overcoming her fears shrouded in an immense dread of vulnerability when asleep seemed inconceivable. No one could ever comprehend that meeting an Illegra in a dream who then physically materialised shattered the divide between nightmare and reality to a point it no longer exists. That simply thinking of a nightmare as something to be quickly forgotten is no longer possible. From the moment the

Illegra came into her reality her perception of the world no longer followed what all humans expected. Dreams themselves were portals to other Dimensions and Realms of reality that up to then had mysteriously eluded her.

Mariam Hope said that she could help. Her confidence clearly evident from her tone and why not Maddox thought. She too had suffered from the supernatural and dealt with others in similar situations. Perhaps she needed something to reach towards, something that offered her the possibility of coming to terms with the most frightening prospect she had ever thought possible. If she ignored Mariam she knew that eventually she would succumb and very possibly kill herself to escape a very real danger. A cold shiver ran up and down her spine causing an involuntary shudder. Never in a million years would she have thought suicide an option she might consider, but her desperation and fear were real as was the threat. Rather than lose her soul to one of those creatures she would rather die. Marian she thought, had her work cut out for her if she was to bring her back from the brink and the unwanted end that she might have to face.

***

Hughes leaned against the front door of the end property expecting to find it locked, instead it swung easily and silently inwards. Confronting them with darkness. A gloomy kind of uninviting murkiness that resisted visibility as if it had something to hide. Ahead stood a narrow hallway dry and still as if it were holding its breath. Hughes sensed the danger. Everything about this place told him to turn around and return to the car. Yet the scream they had heard had sounded female which heightened his natural reaction to help negating everything else. Stepping inside like diving into the sea. The difference immediate. The silence deafening in its intensity. A glance over his broad shoulder at Dukes saw her shadowy figure shrug. That she didn't like it either didn't need words. He took another step into the gloom and almost immediately dropped to his knees under the burden of evil that weighed the air down like an anvil.

Dukes bent beside him curling an arm around his to stop him falling flat onto his face. "What the heck Billy!"

"There's something extremely bad in here," he managed to say propping himself upright on her shoulder.

"Listen," she said. The silence went so deep they could hear their hearts pumping but nothing more, not even the rain hammering down on the sodden ground behind them. "It's like we're in a cocoon."

"I'm okay," he said lifting off her. Abruptly regaining his strength and resuming the lead into the darkness towards the end of the hall. Neither wanted to shine their mobile beams to avoid attracting unwanted attention. Though the possibility that whatever evil lived here already knew they were coming seemed likely. When terrified you try using logic to avoid becoming a victim. It doesn't matter that it slows you down or that your enemy might be invisible and right next to you. You're trying your best satisfying your mind that you're taking necessary precautions. Feeling their way along the hall by following a wall they came across a staircase and navigated around it keeping on the ground floor. What little light there was remained at the front door like a light at the end of a tunnel. No windows gave a hint of moonlight everything was black. Finally Hughes couldn't take it anymore and flicked on his mobile beam fully expecting an Illegra to attack him. Instead he found they had reached the end of the hall and stood at a doorway that led into a kitchen.

Stepping into it brought a fresh set of smells to tease their senses.

Nothing unusual. Vegetables and herbs. A small table dominated the centre of the room while a cooker and cupboards lined the walls. On the table sat a bowl containing a headless unplucked chicken. Its reddish feathers bright in the mobile's beam. A pool of blood surrounded the bowl absorbed by a white tablecloth. Dukes checked the cupboards, but they were empty. No one lived here. How could they she thought.

Moving to a rear window she tried peering outside, but it appeared coated in something that blocked visibility. Keeping together they searched the entire ground floor. A total of four rooms including the kitchen. Nothing. With Hughes staying in front they headed up the stairs. His weight making the boards creak underfoot a warning of their presence. At the top of the stairs sat a landing with four doors. He ran the beam over each in turn stopping at the one at the front of the house. The only one open.

The silhouette of a figure sat in a chair side on to them made Dukes catch her breath. Neither of them moved desperately attempting to pierce the gloom with their eyes. Was it a trap their first thought. The figure remained still giving nothing away.

Moving slowly they crossed the landing towards the figure every sinew and nerve tense as their minds grappled with numerous dark possibilities. The closer they got to the figure the more it became evident it was a man his head slumped away from them. Dukes used her mobile beam to scan the otherwise empty room before they stopped beside the figure and Hughes used one of his huge hands to turn the man's head in their direction. Arthur Burns stared through vacant eyes seeing nothing around him. Not dead but not with them either.

"Burns," Hughes whispered not wanting to disturb the silence more than necessary. "Burns!" He repeated waving a hand in front of his face.

"What's wrong with him?" Dukes asked.

"It's like he's in some kind of trance." Hughes said.

Her beam lit up Burns face revealing a small, fixed smile.

"Whatever he's seeing is making him happy," she said. "Should we call for an ambulance?"

"Not yet," he said. "If he's been left here where is everyone else. Let's find them first I don't think what's happening with him is doing any harm."

They searched the other rooms but found nothing.

"This is bonkers," Dukes said. "We know they're here."

"I think these old places have cellars if they're going to be anywhere it'll be closer to Hell," Hughes said with a grin.

"Is that meant to calm my nerves?" She asked sarcastically.

"I'm here," he reminded her.

"Yeah, and I just helped you from falling over when we stepped into this place. I don't think physical size makes an iota of difference. We're both as vulnerable as one another. Except maybe I run faster."

He led the way back down the stairs without saying more with her close behind. Switching off their lights as they returned to the bottom of the stairs they fumbled along the side of the staircase until Hughes came across a latch that pushed up to release a door which swung out. Inside was black as pitch and Dukes caught Hughes by the arm reluctant to go further without seeing what lay ahead of them.

"They know we're here," she said. "We needs to see where we're going. There will be stairs and we can't afford falling over."

He had intended using his foot to feel for steps but knew she was right even if it meant the others would see them coming. "You think us going down there stupid don't you?"

"I think we've had better ideas," she said.

"Maybe you should stay up here and if anything bad happens get out and warn the others."

"Does that make you feel better saying it because you know I can't let you go in there alone."

He sighed turned on the beam and flashed it over a short landing no more than six by six feet sat on top of an old looking wooden set of stairs that ran down to a stone floor at least twelve feet below. "Wait until I reach the bottom of the stairs and say all clear before coming to join me."

"Whatever you say," she replied.

Stepping through doorways in a property full of supernatural evil was never as straightforward as expected. Hughes was still learning that lesson when he stood on the landing and his legs buckled beneath him, so his knees banged against the small floor with a heavy thud. Next a wave of malevolence so vicious swept up the stairs engulfing him in a tight embrace that made him fear his chest would cave in.

Dukes dropped down beside him without thinking an arm across his broad shoulders. While she loosened his short and tie. "What is it Billy?"

"I've lost all power in my legs," he choked. "Something's squeezing my chest making it hard to breathe."

She felt around his chest without finding anything. Then began reciting the Lord's prayer. Almost immediately he sucked in a lungful of air before passing out.

She rose bending from the waist while trying to pull him by the arm out of the cellar, but found two hundred and twenty-five pounds of dead weight too much.

Something on the stairs hissed. Shining the beam into the cellar she spotted a red mist swirling across the floor gently rising towards her. Time to go she thought and grabbed Hughes by the arm yelling at him to wake up and help her.

The mist slipped onto the landing without sound as it twisted around her ankles. Following the curves of her body as it rose while she struggled with Hughes. With both of them consumed within it she felt a sudden urge to climb down the steps into the cellar. At first she fought it. Yet it quickly grew in strength demanding her obedience until her resistance evaporated and she began the descent.

Too late Hughes came round. Dukes mobile where she had left it on the landing casting its glow into the red mist as she went down to the floor. He called out to her, but she did not look back just kept moving until disappearing out of sight deep into the cellar.

Hughes scrambled through a jacket pocket for his crucifix dragging it out and holding it tightly in front of him. The red swirling mist began to rise once more reclaiming the lower steps before moving upwards. The sense of dread he'd encountered at the front door grew. Swallowing hard his palms turned moist and his forehead filled with rivers of sweat. Repeating the Lord's prayer he closed his eyes as the mist rose just below the landing. Fearful that his soul was about to be sucked from him he kept reciting the prayer while holding the crucifix in front of him. This was not the way he had ever expected to die. Yet ready or not it seemed his time had come. Passing out as the mist touched him even with eyes closed he saw a flash explosion that lit up the cellar. A vague memory when the Hopes arrived and shook him awake.

"Billy," Desmond Hope said his name with obvious concern. "Billy, are you alright?"

His eyes fluttered open revealing the Hopes concerned faces

lit up by torch light. "I...." He sounded hoarse. "Toni," he suddenly remembered. "She went into the red mist in the cellar. I couldn't stop her my legs gave out!"

They stared into the darkness below. Black as pitch. No red mist. Nothing. Hope flashed his torch into it and called out her name. No reply. The cellar remained silent as a grave. "Maybe she returned after you fell unconscious?"

Hughes grim expression reflected that wouldn't have happened. She would never have left him alone on the landing. "I wish I could believe that. They took her. The Satanists."

"Can you stand?" Mariam asked.

His legs moved for the first time tight with cramp but working once more. Pushing himself off the floor with Hope's help they emerged from the cellar into the dark hall. "Arthur Burns is in a bedroom upstairs."

"Arthur," Desmond Hope repeated. "Is he okay?"

"I think so. We left him on a chair. He seemed to be in some kind of trance. Pretty sure he didn't know we were in the room. I thought we'd check out the cellar then take him back with us. I didn't count on losing Toni."

"We can go down and search the cellar," Mariam said. "You stay here."

"No," Hughes said. "I don't know what the red mist is, but it was strong enough to knock me out and take Toni. The same might happen to you two or worse."

"The priests are on their way," she said. "When they arrive we'll search the cellar thoroughly."

Desmond Hope went upstairs and returned moments later, "Arthur has gone. Tell us what you remember?" Hughes told them everything before he passed out which didn't take long. Afterwards, leaning against a wall he phoned Maddox and repeated the story to her. She sympathised, knowing how badly he would feel and chose to join them at the house. The priests arrived a few minutes later and after Hughes repeated the tale again they went down to the cellar. Reciting not the Lord's prayer but something unfamiliar to either Hughes or the Hopes. A dozen priests invaded the cellar floor ready to meet whatever their supernatural enemies possessed as weapons. Hughes and Mariam remained in the hall outside. His legs regaining their strength, but he continued to use the wall for a prop. Suppressing the wish they would find Dukes alive and well. Knowing that she had been taken and may never return had a profound impact on him. Blaming himself only part of it. The red mist and swept over both of them and while it did he had sensed the presence of the Satanists. The humans who had invited the Devil and his hordes of demons and Illegras to their reality. Briefly he had connected with all of them sharing their thoughts in just a heartbeat but long enough to learn their intentions. They believe themselves powerful enough to control the Devil himself.

When the first priest re-emerged from the cellar he joined them wearing a sympathetic expression, "It's empty. Whatever was there is gone."

"Have you ever come across the red mist before?"

Even in the grey darkness his features appeared grim. "Yes," he said flatly.

"What is it?" Hughes asked.

"We believe it to be the portal to Hell itself," he replied. "I'm sorry. Your friend is lost." The house began to shudder as a chant by the priests still in the cellar rose above the sound of creaking timbers and juddering bricks. "They are cleansing the cellar making it impossible to be used again by supernatural entities."

“We should have waited,” Hughes said. “Toni was warned by one of the Black and White spirits not to enter.”

The priest cocked his head suddenly attentive, “She can see the Black and Whites?” He asked

Hughes nodded.

“Did she see them in the cellar?”

The way the priest spoke suggested the Black and Whites were special in some way, but whether that might aid Dukes wasn’t clear. “I have no idea, but why are you asking about the Black and Whites?”

“They are the rarest of spirits for any of us living in this reality to see. Communication with them has as far as I’m aware only occurred on the rarest of occasions with individuals the Church consider as Saints.”

“Toni Dukes a Saint!” Hughes almost laughed, uncertain what to think. “Does that help her?”

"I wish I knew. It is very strange for someone with her ability to be lured to Hell. My understanding is that even the Devil would not want such an individual to contaminate Hell."

"Why is that. You must tell me exactly!" Hughes said lifting off the wall suddenly focused on every detail the priest could offer.

"I can only share what my understanding is," the priest continued. "If she were a Saint Hell would reject her. She would be considered too much of a risk to bring to the core of evil. Her very presence could impact badly on the power of evil, diluting it everywhere."

"Does that mean they'd kill her?"

He shook his head, "Not necessarily. They would not wish to anger the Black and Whites being fearful of reprisals. I suggest it's more likely they would leave her somewhere isolated in the hope she would suffer a natural death."

It was hard for him to imagine Dukes as a Saint, but the possibility and hope the priest provided if true meant that she might still be alive. Finding her however, another issue. Where would they isolate her?

CHAPTER TEN

Maddox arrived at the house while it was still being cleansed by the priests. She found Hughes and the others still in the hall by the cellar door. She felt bad over the loss of Dukes but had no choice other than to show leadership by taking full responsibility. Hoping by doing so it might lighten the load on Hughes broad shoulders. The big detective was taking her loss very badly, blaming himself for not waiting for support before continuing the search. Now he was intent on searching for her on the slimmest of possibilities that she was still alive. Yet with nowhere to even start a search could not be organised, something that he was unwilling to accept.

"We're unlikely to help her by going off half cocked," she told him. "We need help from O'Malley, he might know a way of locating her."

"We should visit Arthur Burns. He was damn well there and might know where they've taken her."

"Look," she said gently touching his hand, "We're still not certain that she's alive. We all hope that she is, but it really is not a certainty. You must bear that in mind not to be disappointed again if she isn't."

He studied her like never before. Knowing how difficult it had been for her to overcome the nightmare of an Illegra climbing out of her dreams. She still hadn't gotten over it and for that reason better than most understood how he was feeling. "I can't believe her to be dead. I need the hope to keep my sanity."

"In a different way so do I," she replied. "I was in charge while Buick is healing. Toni was lost on my watch. You told me what you were intending to do, and I allowed you to place your lives in danger."

"You weren't here," he said. "You reacted to what we described.

Allowing us to check things out was right and proper."

"As was you leading her into that house. You both knew what faced you. You didn't order her to go with you?" It was as much a question as a statement.

He shook his head. "I see what you're doing." She grinned for the first time in days. "You're steering me away from hating myself."

"Hating yourself is a waste of energy. I need you functioning on all cylinders if we're going to find her." She said.

Without doubt she was correct. However, his emotions wanted to move mountains to find her. "Okay, let's do all we can to find her. What do you suggest?"

"We have two leads. The Burns and Dangs. We'll start with those."

"Let's go," he said beginning to turn to leave.

"Tomorrow," she said. "In the morning. You need to get some rest.

Whatever they've done with Toni won't change between then and now."

***

The following morning Buick received news about Dukes disappearance from Maddox. The Superintendent guessed how both Maddox and Hughes were feeling but was glad they were seeking the advice of Father O'Malley before leaving to visit Burns and Dang. Whether either would be home was less certain, but she resisted the temptation to voice her opinion. Keeping themselves occupied necessary to avoid brooding over their loss.

When their call finished she climbed out of bed, dressed, and collected Frobisher on her way out. They had been intending to leave the hospital as both were eager and feeling fit enough to return to work. Filling Frobisher in on what had happened the previous evening as a taxi drove them to the office showed that her young companion also felt the loss. Her short time with IMP had already made her feel a part of a family group. It felt satisfying for Buick to know that.

When they arrived at the office Father O'Malley was already present talking with Maddox and Hughes in the outer office. Buick had purposely not warned them that she would be returning to work that day to avoid any objections the Detective Inspector might have felt necessary to argue. Frobisher went directly to her desk and switched on her computer while making herself comfortable with one arm in a sling.

Buick dropped her satchel onto the floor beside a chair as she sunk back onto it next to the others. Maddox surprised expression required an answer. "We're both well enough to be here and you need someone manning the phones and researching whatever you find when working the streets."

Her excuse sounded both plausible and determined as Commander Brandown stepped into the office.

"Superintendent," he said loudly. "I didn't expect to see you here today."

There are times when being polite tests the best of us. For Buick this was one of those times. She feigned a smile, "Helen and I chose to leave together. We're not much use wasting time at home and the team is one short now, so it makes sense that we return."

"I was going to offer Inspector Maddox a couple of replacements," he said eyeing Father O'Malley. "But if you're certain you can cope I'll leave you to it. Keep me up-to-speed with any progress with finding Sergeant Dukes." Leaving without further discussion no one mentioned him as they returned to listening to O'Malley.

"I was saying Superintendent, that it is unlikely either the Burns or

Dangs returned home. Something very sinister is happening and they would be considered as loose ends if they were caught again."

"What do you believe is going on?" Buick wanted to know.

"The red mist associated with Hell was we believe accessed at the property in Chadwell Heath. As a result the Devil himself has been exposed as playing a significant role in what has happened previously with the Illegras. That can only mean one thing. Armageddon."

"The end of days?" Hughes asked.

"Yes. Look around at what is happening people do not trust the government, corruption within authority is rife. Greed has become an obsession. The rule of law is under threat from those in authority as well as the public. Putin has gone to war with Ukraine and the threat of World War Three is growing by the day."

"I was telling the Farther that when the red mist swept over me I saw into the minds of the Satanists. They think they can control the Devil and use him to control the world."

"That old chestnut," Buick said. "When is anyone going to learn that the Devil is beyond their control."

"Sadly, there is always someone with a better idea of how to go about it. All the while they do the Devil has his own plans and ultimately the destruction of our universe to enrich his own.

"You're making this sound very depressing Father," Maddox said.

"It is what it is Inspector," he replied.

"How might we find Toni?" Hughes asked.

"She's underground. Isolated in a sewer," he replied. The good news lifting their spirits. Dukes was not dead and recoverable.

"You know that for sure?" Buick asked.

"Yes," he said. "But exactly where has not been shared with me."

"Then we're back to square one," Hughes growled angrily.

O'Malley stared at him with understanding, "I can however tell you that she is close to here."

"How close?" Maddox asked.

He shrugged, "Close, spirits don't do measurements."

Buick rose to her feet and moved to her office from which she made a phone call. A few minutes later she returned, "I'm getting a search party organised we'll have every sewer within a mile of here examined. If she's close we'll find her."

Two hours later a hundred officers descended into the London sewers below their offices fanning out in all directions. The sewer network in London dated back to Victorian times with many of the numerous channels remaining untouched since then. The odour was pungent as some officers, those wearing chest high nylon waders pushed through the deepest parts of water with long poles used to prod rubbish as they searched for a body. The search began at midday and by five that evening most of the sewers in the immediate area had been checked without success.

Hughes was in waders with the water level just around his knees when he spotted a light in one of the unused channels with a couple of bricked layers forming a short parapet above the waterline restricting access. The number 10 had been painted in white on the old bricks above the opening. Peering into the darkness with a light at the very end of a long dark dry channel he began climbing the parapet that separated it. Slipping his backside onto its coarse top and swinging his legs over to the other side. His boots touched down on solid dry concrete. Bending his head he moved forward towards the light sensing something in the pungent air other than the stench of waste. Keeping his mouth open he breathed slowly through it avoiding the pungent stench while sensing a hostile presence that grew stronger with every step he took until he came to a halt.

Lifting a microphone from his shoulder he pressed a red button on its top and spoke into the mouthpiece. “This is Inspector Hughes I’m in an unused channel with the number ten painted above it. I can see a light at the end of it and get the impression someone else is down here with me. If any unit is ahead of me and you see my torch light please respond?” Silence. “Hughes to Buick are you receiving over?”

“Loud and clear,” Buick replied from the office.

“Hughes to Maddox, where are you over?” He asked.

“I’ve just found the entrance to channel ten. I’ll be with you in a minute.”

He stood still waiting for Maddox to join him. The channel too narrow for more than a single file which meant he bent at the knees to allow her to see the light ahead of them.

"Doesn't appear to be one of ours," she said.

"That's what worries me," he said. "Look, if I drop to me knees I want you to get the hell out of here. Don't help me just go."

In the dark narrow channel as he turned to look at her for confirmation that she would leave without a second thought the light on his helmet lit her face. For the first time he saw the fear that had burdened her since an Illegra had materialised from her dream. He also saw something else. Genuine concern for his safety. Maddox was not the type to reveal her feelings especially for a work colleague, but one look was obvious enough. He felt the same but now was hardly the time to discuss it. "I'll be alright. Promise."

"I don't like to run away," she said.

"And I don't want us both dying. If whatever that is turns bad someone needs to return to warn Buick and the others."

"Fine," she said her hand holding his arm preventing him from turning away. "But don't die protecting me. My conscience can't stand anymore weight."

"I get it," he said. "Can we go now?"

She released his arm and followed behind. The channel narrowed until it touched either end of Hughes broad shoulders. Maddox wondered if people were smaller in Victorian times as she lost sight of the light ahead unable to see around or over his bulk. Following him for another couple of minutes enough before her patience expired and she asked, "Are we near the light now?"

He stopped and turned sideways so the view of the end of the tunnel was clearly visible. A bright light from above illuminated a dry chamber with chains and shackles fitted to the wall. The light radiated from a large white stone that protruded from the brickwork high above.

“What is this place?” Maddox asked softly.

“Some kind of chamber,” he said turning back and momentarily blocking it from her view before stepping into the chamber following the wall to his left towards another dark passage. “I think people have been imprisoned here,” he said staring at skeletons piled at the edge of the passage.

Standing beside him she looked down, “They’ve been here a long time. This place is a warren there are another three passages going off in different directions.”

“I hope you’re not thinking about splitting up?” He said.

“It would speed things up,” she replied.

He shook his head, "Won't happen. We stay together at all times however long it takes us."

Fine," she said without arguing. "Which passage do you want to search first?"

Stepping over the bones at the nearest passage entrance he went inside with her close behind. Although she would never admit it she was grateful he had stopped her going alone. It was a ridiculous idea given what had happened, but she felt that she had had to suggest it. He stopped just a few steps in.

"What's wrong?" She asked.

"There's nothing this way," he said.

"Are you sure?"

"As sure as I can be," he said. "I can usually feel something when we're headed in the right direction, and this does nothing for me whatever. Let's go back and try another."

They discovered it was the same for the second passage and

returned to the chamber to enter the third and final passage. Immediately they did Hughes felt a surge of energy that undeniably made him catch his breath. "She's here."

There was no light at the end of the passage. No indication there was anything different about it other than Hughes sensitivity. The only illumination came from their helmet torches. The Victorian brick encapsulating them black with age bore deep scratch marks torn so deep it had to have come from an animal. Hughes shone his beam at the marks and pointed.

"That's something you don't see every day."

"Thank heavens," she replied easily imagining the creature responsible. "I think we need to be careful."

He nodded, "I'm getting conflicting sensations. One moment I sense darkness and another something else. Something that I don't understand."

Maddox used her radio and informed Buick what they were doing.

Buick asked, "Do you want back-up?"

Hughes shook his head. Maddox said, "Send it, we'll keep moving. Billy thinks we're close to Toni."

"Be very careful," Buick told them. She didn't want any more officers lost and felt frustrated having to remain at the office instead of accompanying them. Guessing that Maddox must have felt the same didn't help. The trouble with active people is that they have to act. Doing something is their life blood or at least that's how it seems.

From the passage the detectives emerged into a circular chamber. Black as pitch and silent as the grave. Neither of them spoke for some odd reason it seemed inappropriate to do so. The light from their helmets pointed in opposite directions taking in all areas of the chamber until Hughes found a naked figure lying on the stone floor. Tapping Maddox on the arm he pointed to it and slowly moved towards it. Behind him Maddox drew her blade free from a pocket. The face of the woman faced the wall her long grey hair suggesting she was old although her shapely form said otherwise. Hughes kneeled next to her while Maddox surveyed the darkness all round. Turning the woman onto her back revealed it was Toni Dukes. Hair turned grey, but her beautiful face remained as he remembered. Slipping off his waders he removed a jacket and put it around her unconscious form.

“Is she alive?” Maddox asked.

“Yeah,” he said. “She’s breathing but out cold.”

Lifting her off the ground they turned back towards the passage when the squishy plop of things landing in front of them sounded.

Things that had been watching them from the ceiling above. Looking in every direction the lights of their helmets picked out three Illegras blocking the exit. Their arms stretched in front of them with talons glinting wickedly in the beams of light. The fluid shape of the creatures moved continually making their heads neck and torso merge as one before stretching apart in regular motion. Their yellow eyes and toothless mouths the only way of identifying the position of their heads.

The two nearest Hughes stepped towards him talons raised as the detective began reciting the Lord's prayer. Momentarily faltering their momentum just long enough for Maddox to leap between them. Her blade piercing one creature through an eye as the other slashed at her head. The tips of its talons just making contact causing an explosive bright white light that left a puff of smoke where the creature had stood. The

Illegra with her blade in its eye likewise disappeared, but without the bright light, leaving just the one remaining in front of the passage.

"You've lost your protection," Hughes said referring to the prayer they had memorised and repeated on a daily basis. "Take Toni and I'll fend off the last one while you escape."

The creature moved towards her slashing and slicing the air as she dodged and dived out of its reach. "No time Billy. Get her out of here."

"I won't leave you," he shouted.

"Get Toni out of here!" Maddox said.

"I can't leave you," he said fearfully.

"Damn it Billy take her out. I'll keep this thing busy!"

With Dukes cradled in his arms and the Illegra slashing right and left any hope of returning her to the floor and joining Maddox in the fight was quickly forced out of his head. He didn't want this. Didn't want to leave

Maddox behind as he rushed to the passage without looking back. Moving quickly through the darkness listening to the sound of battle behind him. As he reached the end of the passage a group of uniformed officers appeared. Handing her over to them he ordered they take her out. Ordered that none follow him back into the passage. Then he was running. Racing through the darkness again the light from his helmet bouncing off the black surroundings he shouted to warn Maddox of his return. Praying that she could keep the creature from killing her. Eager to reach her in time. As he cannoned from the passage blade at the ready his beam found Maddox standing alone. Jacket and waders ripped. Blood running down her face.

"I killed it," she said turning to him. A small smile expressing surprise.

He stopped in front of her. Face full of incredulity turning quickly to relief. Grabbing her swiftly into his powerful arms he gave her a bear hug that might have done more damage than the Illegra. “Thank God!”

After being released she sucked in a deep breath as her ribs returned to normal. “That made up for the nightmares they’ve given me.”

“We’d better get back. Some uniforms took Toni to the surface.”

CHAPTER ELEVEN

It was the next day when Buick visited Dukes at the hospital meeting a doctor in her room she asked for an update on her officer's condition.

"She's in a coma. We're recording minimal brain activity. Fortunately, she's able to breathe without assistance. All we can do is maintain observation and hope she will naturally wake."

It was an unsatisfactory answer, but not unexpected. Buick used a seat alongside her bed as the doctor left them alone. With the bleep of a monitor the only sound in the room she reached and placed her hand on Dukes hand. Closing her eyes as she recited a prayer:

'Father God, we pray for our colleague Toni Dukes to return to us. We give thanks for the incredible NHS staff here in the UK. Lord would you sustain and keep them during

these difficult times. Grant nurses, doctors, and other health professionals great wisdom as they make medical decisions about our colleague Toni Dukes. Help them help her to return to us. We need her.

Father God, we praise you for supporting our efforts against the Devil and his disciples. We give thanks for the incredible efforts and expertise of those who have fought with us. We pray that you would continue to grant those who support us the necessary insight and strength as they continue to defend our world. Amen.

Buick remained at her bedside for a further half hour before rising to return to the office. As she turned from the bed Dukes sighed loudly arresting Buick's attention. The monitor's bleep accelerated, as a blinking red light above a screen remained on. Buick stood by the bedside as a doctor and two nurses entered the room at a rush. Backing away close to a window watching the medical staff at work.

Dukes eyes fluttered open staring up at the doctor and nurses surrounding her, “Where am I?”

“You’re at hospital. You were unconscious when they found you. How are you feeling?” The doctor said.

Dukes pushed herself up on elbows and spotted Buick by the window, “Boss!”

She came forward surprise on her face. Dukes eyes had changed from dark to grey same as her hair. How she would react when she saw herself for the first time Buick dared not guess. “You’ve been through a lot Toni.”

“I feel fine,” she said throwing the covers aside while attempting to climb out. A nurse stopped her putting the covers back in place.

“You need to remain here for observation,” the doctor insisted.

"But I feel fine," she repeated.

Buick rummaged in her satchel to find a mirror which she handed to Dukes. "Take a look at yourself."

She did just that and screamed explosively, "Ooh my god! My hair, my eyes what happened to me?"

She stared at Buick for an explanation. The Superintendent asked the doctor and nurses to give them a moment and waited while they vacated the room. "You were taken by a red mist that we believe is directly associated with the Devil."

She frowned trying to recall but nothing other than fuzzy memories of Hughes on his knees at the top of the landing returned. "I don't remember a thing after Hughes collapsed on the landing. What happened to him?"

"He's fine. You were the only one taken. Together with Bran he rescued you from a sewer where you were being held by three Illegras."

"But why did they change the colour of my hair and eyes?"

It occurred to her to suggest that O'Malley and the priests believed she might be a Saint but decided against it given her reaction to the physical changes she already had to accept. Being considered Saintly might be more than she could currently cope with. "If the doctors think you can leave tomorrow I'll come and collect you."

"I feel fine now, even with this awful colour disfiguring me," she said and immediately regretted it as Buick had recently lost her arm. "Sorry, Boss. Didn't mean to be cruel."

"Forget it. I know what your appearance means to you." She said. "Remain here tonight, let the doctors check you out. When you get back to us we'll have a lot to discuss."

"How's Helen?"

"Back at work. She and I are make IMP appear as a dangerous place to be," she laughed.

Her laugh refreshing to hear Dukes thought. "Thanks for being here Boss."

“You’re important to everyone at IMP. Never forget that” she told her.

***

The following morning Buick arrived at the hospital around ten with Hughes and Maddox accompanying her, eager to see Dukes. The doctors had given the detective a clean bill of health and she was eager to be out of the hospital as soon as she possibly could. As the three arrived in the room to collect her they found Dukes making gestures with her hands.

“Is a Black and White here?” Hughes asked.

Dukes nodded unwilling to be distracted by their arrival, “He wants to help us.”

“How?” Buick asked.

“He knows where they’ve taken the portal,” she said without turning away from the spirit at the end of her bed. “He’ll take us to it.”

It took Buick two hours to arrange for the support needed to challenge whatever they might meet at the red mist portal. With Dukes leading them following the spirit they arrived outside the House of Lords.

"He says it's in the basement," Dukes said. Behind Buick and her team were the Hopes, O'Malley and more than a hundred priests, rabbis, and clergy from across London. It was an army the likes of which London had never seen.

It may have been appropriate Buick thought that an early eighteenth-century parliamentary building was to be used by the Devil to access our reality. The centre of a human government a preferred choice as it reflected the overall intention of a supernatural deity to stamp its mark on the people of a nuclear power. The establishment of a foothold in our reality demonstrated to the entire world the truth of their existence. No longer would the Devil be considered fiction as his armies swarmed across continents overwhelming all opposition. After awareness was fully accepted by every living human the reality in which humans existed would implode after the mining reached the Earth's core and was flooded by energy from the other dimension. Nothing would survive. No memory of their being or passing. Of course it would take time.

Although not a serious historical buff she recalled reading that in 1649 the House of Lords was abolished by an act of Parliament that claimed the House of Lords was useless and dangerous to the people of England. It was not reinstated until 1660. Today, it was indeed dangerous to the people of the entire globe.

A tall arch made from sand coloured stone occupied by a pair of armed police officers stood ready to greet Buick's army. Flashing her ID to the officers they stepped aside allowing the procession to feed in through glazed wooden doors onto a large open marble floor. A security officer approached them, and Buick explained they had an urgent need to be led to the basement.

The security officer gave her a strange look but nodded and asked them to follow him. Old buildings of the period often possessed concealed routes to various rooms within their structure. The access via a door that initially appeared as part of a wall was no different to expectations. It led below the catacombs, below those buried for hundreds of years. The security officer was instructed to remain by the door to prevent anyone following and to remain there until they returned.

Buick with O'Malley led the way down a long spiral stone stairwell with small lights overhead. More than a hundred footsteps announcing their descent. Where the overhead lighting stopped they continued on following the beams from their mobiles. The darkness intensifying the echo of their footsteps.

"How deep does this go," Dukes asked Maddox at her side.

"We passed the catacombs a few minutes ago. Seems like we're going straight to Hell."

"Don't even joke about it," Dukes said.

More time passed before the stairwell finally ended. Ahead and all around an impenetrable pitch black that deflected torchlight. Casting their beams in every direction to no avail did not bode well.

"I have an idea, "O'Malley said gesturing to three priests and Mariam to join him.. "I want you three to go off in different directions. Mariam I want you to remain with us and describe what each of them sees. We will form a phalanx and continue in a straight line. A chalk line will be drawn along the ground from here showing our progress. If any of you become disorientated Mariam will be able to help you find us again."

"Guess I'm glad I'm not a priest," Dukes muttered.

As they headed off in different directions O'Malley ordered the priests to form a phalanx and begin reciting a prayer. Mariam closed her eyes as her brother took her hand to steer her as they moved. The sound of their footfalls like a co-ordinated military unit.

"Their prayer should shield us from Illegras and lesser entities," O'Malley said.

Buick nodded, even though his reassurance did not reduce the tension she felt. They were about to confront the Devil himself. For the first time she wondered how prayers and a few humans could hope to defeat a deity. What they had been doing over the past few years fighting evil suddenly appeared nought by comparison. Also, the hand she had lost ached as if it were still attached while the stub of her arm kept giving involuntary twitches. Just when she needed to focus the loss of her left hand began to complain!

“We’re getting near something bad,” Hughes said suddenly. His deep voice easily overwhelming the marching step of the priests.

O’Malley called a halt and as one the priest behind them stopped even the Grenadier Guards would have been envious

A moment later Mariam gasped, “I think one of the priests has found something.”

“The red mist?” Buick asked.

She shook her head, “No. A creature moving in the darkness. Not an Illegra. Something else.”

“In which direction?” Maddox asked.

“Straight ahead,” she replied. “He’s reciting the Lord’s prayer and holding up a crucifix.” She paused the seconds feeling like minutes as they waited. “I’m not sure what’s happening his vision is blurring,” she said with concern. “His eyes furiously blinking. I think he's passing out. I no longer see through his eyes."

Hughes took off at a run towards the priest ahead of them.

"Damn it," Buick said.

"He can't help himself when someone's in trouble," Maddox said.

"We must continue," O'Malley said as they began their slow walk following in Hughes wake.

"What's happening with the other two?" Buick asked Mariam.

She frowned the pupils behind her closed eyes making abrupt movements as if she were attempting to follow something. "I can't see through either of them. They're gone."

A blast of hot air suddenly swept across the ground lashing at their faces with dust and forcing the priests to stop their prayer. O'Malley gestured for everyone to kneel down and cover their heads as the wind screamed as if in torment. Minutes later it stopped as abruptly as it had begun. The silence that followed deathly quiet as a tomb. Impossible to ignore. Rising to their feet the priests began to pray. The chant of their voices shattering the silence in a way that made it feel it was resisting them.

Buick was certain about one thing. Red mist or not they were where the Devil wanted them to be. The ground beneath their feet began to tremble and shake just enough to make everyone lower their stance at the knee to compensate. Keeping upright felt the best possible stance right then. Being able to run at short notice most on Buick's mind.

"What's happening?" Maddox asked.

"The Devil is coming," O'Malley answered. "Have your blades ready and stay behind me. He will appear soon."

This was it then Buick thought. Her stump shook before twisting in a circular movement she had no power to control. It moved with a will of its own nothing she did could stop it.

O'Malley leaned close, "Don't resist, let it happen."

"Let what happen?" She asked as the stump accelerated and became invisible. Watching it she caught her breath as something began to emerge something that glowed with a golden aura. The spinning stump slowed to a halt and her eyes went wide at the sight of a glowing lower arm and hand.

"You have received the Hand of God," O'Malley told her.

She turned the hand over and studied it's large palm and thick fingers. It was at least three sizes too big for her, but she could feel its power and energy streaming through her entire body. Any doubts she had felt dissipated its presence giving her the confidence to achieve the impossible.

The ground just ahead of them fell away in the fashion of a sink hole. No one moved no one spoke. All waited for the inevitable figure of the Devil to appear.

A red mist rose from the sink hole and Hughes sucked in a breath of air as if starved of oxygen. “He’s coming!”

The mist came over the top of the sink hole and in a very narrow band stopped just ahead of them thickening as it did so. The atmosphere felt suddenly strained as the priests continued to chant while Buick and O’Malley stepped forward.

The mist began to dissipate as a small figure emerged from it. A child no older than ten in appearance. Wearing a dark top and trousers. Dark hair parted on the right. His ashen features and dark eyes handsome yet menacing at the same time.

A cold shiver flushed over Buick as she recognised him. The boy the mirror image of her sister’s dead son. What game was the Devil playing?

“It is my time,” he said.

“No,” O’Malley replied. “It most definitely is not!”

The boy tilted his head to the side changing his expression to one of curiosity. Studying the priest then Buick and the golden hand that glowed from her left arm. "I have waited long enough."

"The Lord says you must go back," O'Malley said.

The boy moved forward, and they both felt his energy clash against the shield created by the prayers. It was the first time Buick realised a defence shield could be made visible when encountering an enemy energy. "Do you suppose their prayers can resist me if I decide to reach in and snatch either of you?" As he spoke so his hand pushed through the energy barrier crackling and spitting as it did so. Tiny sparks of electricity bounced off the child's hand as his pointed finger stopped just short of O'Malley.

Buick acted instinctively using the golden hand to shove the child's hand away, back behind the shield. The boy yelped snatching his hand from her grip revealing burnt flesh where she had touched him. Staring back at her his gaze grew dark. A darkness that she felt like a slap across the face. Momentarily staggering backwards she caught herself. Don't meet his gaze she told herself. Focus on his torso. Human nature tells us to meet the gaze of others when communicating, a characteristic that human enemies use to good effect.

"Why have you come to us with the appearance of that child?" Buick asked.

"Does my appearance disturb you?"

"Is that what you hoped?"

"I hoped that we could come to a mutually beneficial agreement," he said.

"I don't see how that's possible given your end game is the end of our universe."

"An inevitability that you wish to delay," he replied. His tone melodic as if singing the words. “Why do you resist the inevitable. I do not understand?”

“If God wanted us destroyed I’m sure he wouldn’t have provided us this,” she said raising the Hand of God.

The boy smiled but not in a nice way. His dark eyes flashing with momentary anger before settling down to something less aggressive. “You think the Hand of God can prevent your destruction, but not even it has the power to prevent that from happening.”

Buick frowned uncertainly. The surge of power she felt when the arm appeared continued to race through her body pushing doubts aside. “You think you can lie to win us over, but we know your games?”

“Do you? Why would I need to lie,” he said. “Your position is hopeless. He knows that as well as I do. He provided the Hand to deceive you, it appears he was successful.”

"What you claim doesn't make sense. If you really are the Devil then we should expect everything you say to be a lie."

The boy glanced over his shoulder and gestured with a hand. From the moody darkness behind a pair of demons materialised with Hughes held tightly between them. Behind them members of the Satanic Chapel led by Emily Burns. They moved around the sink hole forcing Hughes to stand in front of them. "Your friend arrived too late to save the priest."

Maddox stepped forward with a gasp.

Buick touched her arm to calm her before turning back to the boy. "Will you release him?"

"You care about him," the boy remarked. "Your emotions give you all away. They are a weakness of the human species. The woman next to you has the deepest concern for his safety." Turning to look down the sink hole he continued, "Perhaps I'll send him to my home for the flesh to be torn from his body." With a quick look at Maddox he sneered at her distress. "You are pitiful creatures."

Buick ignored hm, "If you're as powerful as you think then returning him to us will add nothing to our attempt to stop you."

The boy studied her for several minutes before answering, "No, but you misunderstand me. There is no need for us to fight and I will show you why if you permit me to do so. All I need is your agreement to give me the opportunity."

Only Dukes spotted the Black and White spirits appear to the left of the boy. Their appearance unexpected she sensed they did not want her to inform the others of their presence. Watching them in stunned silence she held her breath as they formed a line behind the boy. Hovering above the sink hole as the red mist rose from it to greet them.

"Don't agree to anything," O'Malley said.

"It's alright Father, "she replied. "Trust me."

"I will let you have your opportunity, but you must promise that should I decline your offer you will leave us in peace and close this portal."

"You have my word," the boy said.

It wasn't easy to talk with a child who she knew to be dead for the past two years. Someone who she had loved dearly and enjoyed talking and playing with. The Devil was indeed cunning using his image to taunt her. Freddie had been a wonderfully exuberant boy so full of life always dreaming about a future he would never know. He drowned while on holiday with his parents. His body never recovered.

"Do you wish to call me by this child's name?" The Devil asked.

Damn she thought. He read my mind! “Stay out of my head!”

“I sensed your sadness, it’s very powerful. However, I will not read you again.” With that in a flash her surroundings changed. No longer were they underground standing in front of a huge sink hole. Now she stood on a flat white floor with a white sky and infinite white featureless horizon. Beside her the IMP team appeared as mystified as she was.

“What’s happening?” She asked.

The boy remained standing in front of her a charming smile parting his lips. “This is the opportunity I asked for,” he said. “This is what I can offer you in return for letting me do what is inevitable.”

“Get on with it!” She said irritated that he had been able to snatch them away from O’Malley and the others so easily. It revealed his power and their weakness which was what he had wanted. Why he had felt it necessary to play out this farce a mystery?

"There is no need for you or any of your friends to die. You can live out your lives here in my world. You will have everything you ever dreamed about around you."

"He's making it sound very attractive," Dukes said.

"I'm sorry, but the destruction of our world and universe isn't for sale."

"I've only just begun to list what my offer has," the boy remarked as he gestured to his left and a group of people materialised. "All the people you have loved throughout your life will be returned for the duration of your life in my dimension."

Her parents, their parents and other friends and family stood together waving and smiling. A sharp intake of breath caught in her throat making her cough helping her suppress an urge to return the wave.

"Rather than simply stop to exist you can have the remainder of your life spent with all your familiars," he told her.

Each of the IMP team also stared at a collection of friends and family who had passed on. Now standing in front of them hoping to be noticed as they furiously waved in their directions.

"What's the alternative?" Hughes asked.

"You already know that. You will cease to exist same as the rest of the people on your planet. The human race is about to be eliminated would you not rather collect more enjoyable memories before that happens to you?"

"I would," Maddox said.

Buick shot a look at her shocked that she of all people would be swayed by what the Devil offered. Death always at the end of it, and worse the end of humanity. It was unlike Maddox to choose herself over anyone else. In fact it was odd for any of her team to make that choice.

She studied the boy. His charming smile and innocence almost convincing her of his candour. But this boy was not the individual she had known he was the Devil cloaked in human skin and as such possessed no scruples or inhibitions. He could and would lie until he achieved his aim. Glancing back at the others she guessed what was happening and who they really were.

"Take me back," she told him and felt a surge of energy return to her left arm.

"You are making a grave mistake," the child told her.

"My only mistake was thinking that you could be trusted to make an offer that I might agree. Wiping out humanity was never a possibility as far as I'm concerned. You knew that."

"Then you will die with the rest of your species," he replied coldly dark eyes turning jet black.

"Take me back. If I'm to die then I wish to be with them when I do."

"Very well," he agreed. In a heartbeat they returned to O'Malley and the others.

"Where were you Boss?" Maddox asked.

"No matter. He can't be trusted." She said wondering if she would ever get the opportunity to tell them she had met their duplicates on another plain.

"Well, I guess he is the Devil so it kinda fits," Hughes remarked.

The boy child stood at the front of the huge sink hole arms outstretched as he conjured up the armies of Hell. The roar of thunder and bellows of rage rose from the sink hole ahead of thousands of demons and Illegras as they rushed up the side of the hole, their hooves and feet hammering the ground. Only Dukes saw the Black and White spirits join hands as they hovered over the hole with a thickening red mist enveloping them. Yet none looked perturbed by its touch. In fact quite the opposite she thought.

Behind Buick the priests began their chant raising their voices to the fullest to increase the defence offered by their prayer. As if possessing a mind of its own her golden arm reached out stretching more than thirty feet for its hand to grab the boy child around the waist and lift him into the air above the sink hole. Beneath him the demons and Illegras appeared clawing their way up from the depths of whatever pit they had dwelt. A blinding white and blue band of energy suddenly shone down from the Black and White spirits. The band swaying right and left as demons and Illegras arrived and disappeared in puffs of black smoke. The horde of evil entities kept coming. Thousands at a time. Climbing onto the level ground before fragmenting into oblivion. For more than an hour the uneven battle continued until no others dared expose themselves to the relentless energy.

Buick had held the boy child above the sink hole all the while even as he changed form turning back to the Devil he truly was. A red scaley skinned beast with horns and tail. Raising the creature high the arm hurled the Devil into the depths of the sink hole. The throw so powerful it generated a blast of hot air that threw everyone except Buick to the ground. For more than a minute the ground shook so mightily no one was able to regain their footing before the sink hole disappeared as if it had never existed.

In an instant the demons holding Hughes vanished in puffs of smoke while the Satanists fled the way they had come. All except Arthur Burns who collapsed on the ground unable to move.

No one gave the Satanists chase. They could be collected at another time. Their pact with the Devil finished.

Buick's golden arm disappeared in front of her eyes leaving cinders of memory that made her feel good about herself and what they had achieved.

Turning to O'Malley she smiled as he spoke.

"The portal is destroyed. The Devil has been rejected by God."

She nodded her expression surprisingly serene after the ordeal she had just experienced.

"We won?" Dukes asked as if uncertain. Tucking her long grey hair behind her ears.

O'Malley nodded, "The natural balance is restored. For now."

THE END

Other Novels in the Betty Buick Series

The Underground Mystery

The Next Teen

Printed in Great Britain
by Amazon

38334230R00225